All Max O'Rourke ever wanted was to be a cop. All Tommy LeBarre ever wanted was to play his beloved piano. As a jazz player in one of Storyville's finest bordellos, Tommy is happy. Until the cops raid the place, arresting everyone. But Tommy is the real prize, and Max knows it. Someone wants Tommy gone, if not dead. Taking Tommy in to keep him safe puts Max's career and life on the line, not to mention coming clean about his desire for Tommy. Both men have a lot to lose, but if they can survive they might have everything to gain.

To Jennifer

Lynn Lorenz

2019

Storyville

Lynn Lorenz

MLR PRESS

Published by
MLR Press, LLC
3052 Gaines Waterport Rd.
Albion, NY 14411

Visit ManLoveRomance Press, LLC on the Internet:
www.mlrpress.com

Cover Art by Trace Edwards
Editing by Kris Jacen

eBook format also available
Print ISBN # 978-1-64122-271-6

SECOND EDITION Issued 2017

Trademarks Acknowledgment

The author acknowledges the trademark status and trademark owners of the following wordmarks mentioned in this work of fiction:

Picayune: NOLA Media Group

Chapter One

New Orleans, 1916

I'd been a cop walking a beat since I was nineteen. Nothing I ever wanted to do but be a cop. I'm Irish. It was cop, fireman, or bartender, but my dad was a cop, so there you have it.

I'd been assigned to Storyville since I was twenty-seven, almost three years ago. In all that time, I'd gone with the flow, like the flotsam and jetsam in the muddy waters of the river running past this city headed to the gulf. If my captain said no busts in Storyville, I'd lay off. If he said go break some heads, I'd swing my baton.

Like a good cop. It's all I'd ever wanted.

Until I stepped through the doors of The Pleasure Palace and caught sight of Tommy LeBarre playing that beat-up upright piano. I'd never wanted anyone so much. And I knew wanting him was so far out of line, so far over the edge of fucked up, that if I ever crossed that line, there'd be no turning back. Not for me.

Not for a good cop.

So I stuffed my want down deep. Kept listening to Tommy play that piano—jazz they called it—through the open windows of the Palace. Kept pushing him outta my head, and outta my cock and my balls, where the want for him was so bad it hurt.

And kept walking my beat.

"I heard there's talk about shutting Storyville down," I told James

Stoli, my wop patrol partner, as we strolled down Basin Street.

That's right—an Italian and an Irishman. We made quite a pair. Both of us were second generation. His parents could barely speak English, and if you count the thick Irish accent, neither did mine. New Orleans was changing; it was no longer just French and Spanish. Immigrants were moving in, changing neighborhoods, like the Irish Channel down around Magazine Street, where my parents lived.

His family lived off Esplanade behind the Vieux Carre. Lots of Italians there.

So, you see, James and I had more in common than you might think, us two cops on this beat.

All around us, Storyville came to life, rising out of the dusk. We passed old Joe at the top of his ladder lighting the streetlamp and raised our batons to him. He nodded as he swung the glass door shut.

"Never. Too many of the hoi-poloi have Blue Books." James tapped his chest pocket where he kept his own copy of that little book describing Storyville's most talented ladies of the night. Used to call them soiled doves, but here in Storyville, these doves were more like peacocks and their houses no cheap saloons, but well decorated salons where New Orleans' rich and famous played.

The door to the Brown Pelican opened, and a woman stepped outside. She pulled a dark red flowered dressing gown around her, lit a cigarette, and inhaled deeply. "Hi, boys," she drawled. Her whiskey-roughened voice and southern accent could excite even the most straight-laced men.

James answered, "'Evening, Miss Lavidia." He doffed his hat to her. It worked on him, not me, but I gave her a polite nod.

"Coming 'round later?"

He gave me a quick look, then said, "Sure. Tell Miss Victoria I'll be by after my shift." Not for the first time I wondered if I should say something about James' fancy for Miss Victoria, a mulatto whore he'd fallen for hard.

We all knew nothing could come of it, but that didn't stop James from giving it to her every chance he got. For a fee. Miss Victoria might have liked James, but she was still a whore and still charged him, just like all the others.

Another thing James and I had in common. We were both in love with the wrong person.

Miss Lavidia winked, finished her cigarette, and then stubbed it out on the cement steps of the large house. Ever since the Chicago fire, people were more careful.

James puffed up and twirled his baton on its leather strap. I hated when he did that—made him look like pompous ass. Not that he wasn't, but I had to walk next to him.

Old Joe had carried his ladder on to the next lamp on the street.

Across the street, at The Pleasure Palace, music floated out of the open windows. My mouth went dry and my cock took notice. Tommy had started playing early.

My partner caught my frown. "Don't you like jazz?" James asked.

"Not really. Why?"

"Nothing." He walked on, keeping up with my longer strides. "It's just that whenever we pass the Palace, and the music is playing, you get…so…tense."

For a second, fear coursed through me. Had James figured it out? Had I let my guard down? Had he seen something in me? Something between me and Tommy?

"Well, it makes me nervous. I like a nice slow waltz," I lied. In truth, I liked jazz. Especially what came out of one particular piano. However, I didn't want James in on that. Even if he was my partner, even if I knew about his love for a whore, I didn't trust him enough to tell him my darkest secret.

I glanced over at the Palace. Tommy would be sitting, hunched over the keyboard, his foot working the pedals of the old black upright, his slim, strong fingers dancing over the ivories, lost in making that music.

Last time I was in there on a routine call, he looked up at me, smiled, and I about lost control. "Hi ya, Max!" He didn't even stop playing to talk to me. "Bust any heads today?" He always asked me that. Every time. I always said, "Not yet."

Then I'd get the hell outta there before I said something more.

I fixed my gaze on the street in front of me, determined I'd not go in there tonight. Not without cause. Too many visits and it'd be suspicious. And I didn't want anyone asking me questions I didn't have the answers to. Or the wrong answers.

So we kept walking.

As the sun set, both horse drawn wagons and those new pickup trucks jostled for positions in front of the rows of houses lining each side of Basin. Deliverymen and houseboys of all colors carried barrels of beer and crates of hooch into the houses. Negro maids, dressed in black uniforms with white aprons and little white lace caps, stood on the stoops, and ordered them about, pointing and shouting. Old gray-haired Negro men with push brooms and buckets of soapy water cleaned the banquettes in front of the houses of the filth from the previous night and day.

In just a few hours, Basin Street and the rest of Storyville would come to life. Carriages and automobiles carrying New Orleans' finest gentlemen, dressed in black tuxedos and white gloves, would arrive. They'd descend from their vehicles and enter whichever house they'd chosen to spend the evening in, being entertained by New Orleans' finest whores.

And James and I, two of New Orleans' police force, would just keep walking our beat, making sure those fine upstanding citizens were safe and no trouble broke out on the street. Or occasionally we'd be called into the houses to remove some gentleman too deep in his cups and safely escort him home or to his club to sleep it off.

No one got arrested. Not anyone of standing, if you get my drift.

Storyville paid a lot to city hall for protection, and in return, city hall told the force to turn a blind eye. Everyone knew it. It was no secret. Even the newspapers reported on who'd been seen where and with whom. Just like on the society pages of the *Picayune.*

Frankly, I didn't give a damn one way or the other. I wasn't ever going to find myself in one of the houses looking for a good time. I didn't have the money, first. Second, women were not where I found my pleasure, and third, Storyville wasn't where I'd go to find it.

There were dark alleys and sloe-eyed, coffee-skinned young men on Rampart Street. Boys who'd let a man do just about anything for the right price. I knew. I'd been.

Being caught on Rampart Street would end my career as a copper and my hopes of making detective one day. I only went when the need drove me and that wasn't often these days. I didn't have much, but I still had my dreams.

I stole another look at the Palace over my shoulder. I squashed the foolish thought that tonight we might be called in there and I'd catch a glimpse of Tommy, his blond hair, parted in the middle, falling into his face and covering those thick glasses he wore, playing on that piano and my soul.

§ § § §

At ten that evening, James and I had circled back to Basin Street. An hour left on our shift, then James could see Miss Victoria. And me? Well, Rampart Street would still be there if I dared.

A black paddy wagon turned the corner, two coppers hanging off the running boards on either side of the front doors and two on the back bumper. I put a hand on James's arm. "Wait. What's going on?"

"A raid?" James looked as puzzled as I felt.

"No raids in Storyville. Chief's orders." I didn't know what was happening, but whatever it was, I didn't like it. It stank like three-day-old fish on ice.

The wagon pulled up outside The Pleasure Palace. My heart stopped. Tommy was in the Palace. His music filled the night air, competing with the music coming from one of the houses on the other side of the street, as their trumpet player blew his lungs out.

"Let's go!" I took off, racing down the banquette, trying to beat the other coppers inside. James followed, and we managed to join them as they entered.

"Raid! Everyone line up!" one of the first coppers in shouted.

Pandemonium broke out. Women screamed. Gentlemen politely protested. Cops scattered, snatching scantily dressed women from men's laps, and through it all, Tommy played jazz.

James ran up the stairs after some gent, and I fought my way to the piano. The little fool hadn't run for it. Didn't have the good sense God gave him to head for the back door. What was he waiting for?

I slid up next to the piano. "What the hell are you doing?" Someone threw a vase and it smashed into the wall above the piano. Glass shards rained down on the keyboard.

Tommy cursed and pulled his hands back, looking at the pieces of blue-and-white Chinese pottery covering the ivories. He looked up at me, tossing his hair out of the way. Behind his glasses, owlish blue eyes blinked at me in surprise.

"What?"

"It's a raid." I grabbed Tommy's elbow, pulling him up and away. "Come on, boy. Let's get you out of here."

"But my piano!" He reached for it, as if he could put it in his pocket.

"Forget it. You can't play piano in jail." I half dragged him down the back hall, past a few still-shut doors. Inside, I'm sure the patrons and their doves were scrambling to get dressed and out the ground floor windows.

Tommy had dug in his heels, as if we would go back for the piano. Did he expect me to lug it on my back? I'm big, but not that big.

"Let go of me!" He still struggled.

Now I was getting pissed. We reached the end of the hall. The back door stood open, the kitchen staff and maids having already made their escapes. I swung Tommy around and threw him up against the wall.

I pressed my body up against his, my forehead touching his.

"Listen, you little idiot. The cops are going to arrest everyone. Everyone. And who's going to make your bail?"

He looked up at me, eyes slightly crossed behind thick glasses. "You, Max?" Then a shy smile played on his lips. The tip of his pink tongue flashed over his upper lip.

Damn, I wanted him.

"Hey, you!" a voice called from the head of the hallway. I jerked away from Tommy and looked up. The copper started our way. "Is that the piano player? Cap'n said to make sure we bring him in," he shouted.

"I got him! Little bastard was trying to get out the back," I called out, grabbing Tommy by the arm and twisting it behind him. Why the hell would they want the piano player? He wasn't breaking any laws, unless they'd made jazz illegal.

Tommy cried out in pain, and God forgive me, my prick stiffened.

"Get him in the wagon!" the cop called back and turned away to chase after someone else.

That was my cue to get the hell outta there.

I quick marched Tommy to the back door and kicked the screen door open. A set of wooden steps led down to a dark small yard. On the right, breaking the darkness, a gate to the back alley stood open.

"Let's get you out of here." I pushed him down the stairs, and he was moving on his own now.

Tommy looked back at me and glared as he rubbed his arm. Light from the doorway illuminated his face. "I need my piano."

"Look. It's fine in there. They're not going to take it. Now can we get out of here?"

He put his hands on his hips. "Where?"

He had me there. "Your place?"

He pointed to the house. "That *is* my place. I live there."

"At the Palace?" *Well, hell.* Never knew that.

"Yeah. I have a room. It's not much, but…it's mine." He jutted out his chin, daring me to say anything

"Okay. Not here."

Shouts from the front of the house echoed as they loaded up the paddy wagon. Someone would realize the kid was missing and come looking. Meanwhile, I stood in the dark yard, arguing with a wet-behind-the-ears twenty-year-old piano player who twisted me up like my grandmother's yarn.

"My place." It was all I could think of. I swear on Jesus, Joseph, and Mary. With all the commotion of the raid, I knew James would cover for me back at the station.

He stared at me, bit his bottom lip, and then nodded. "Okay. Your place."

I led the way, and Tommy followed. We reached the gate, and I stuck my head out to see if it was clear. Toward the front, the lights from the street shone as shadows of men and women played over the walls of the house next door. No way could we just step out of the alley there without being seen.

The other way looked better—more darkness to hide in. The street at the end was Crozat. Not much there. "This way." I jerked my head for him to follow. Amazingly, he did and without protest.

That meant I had no reason to put my hands on him.

Chapter Two

After making our way down Crozat toward the St. Louis Cemetery, we reached St. Louis Street and turned back up to Basin. I flagged down a carriage and gave him my address in the Fouburg Marginy, on the other side of the old Vieux Carre. Tommy climbed up, then I got in next to him and shut the door.

We rode in silence, Tommy fuming, arms crossed over his chest, and me glaring out the window.

"Frenchman!" The cabbie shouted, and the horse came to a halt.

I threw open the door, got out, and almost reached for Tommy, to help him down. He jerked away from me, his gaze darting up to the cabbie.

Got it.

I dug into my trousers and pulled out a dollar coin, then tossed it up to the cabbie. He caught it, gave me a nod of thanks, and snapped the reins over the back of the horse. As he took off, we watched for a moment.

"Inside," I whispered. Sound echoed at night, and I wasn't interested in my neighbors knowing I'd brought a man to my house.

Tommy gave me a frown and stomped through the little iron gate, down the brick walk, and up the wooden steps. He waited at the door of the shotgun, arms folded, dark gaze pinned on me.

I took my time getting to the door, pulling my key out, putting it in the lock, turning it, and opening the door, just to keep my hands from shaking. I stepped to the side. "Come in."

He did and moved to the center of the nearly empty room. I turned up the gas lamp near the door, enough to let us see without bumping into what furniture I did own.

"This is yours?" he asked, looking around.

"Yeah. I pay the rent." I shrugged, taking off my police cap and tossing it to the hat rack. It caught the hook and swung there.

"Nice." He grinned. "The trick with the hat."

I rolled my eyes. "You can sleep on the couch. I'm guessing the Palace will reopen in a few days."

"Sure." He nodded and walked to the couch. "I suppose you don't have an extra set of pajamas or a night shirt."

"Right." I made my way down the side hall running from front door to back door, passing the small kitchen, an even smaller bathroom, to my bedroom in the back. I turned up a lamp and went to the armoire. After digging through one of the drawers, I found something he could wear.

"What is it?"

I jumped. My heart galloped as I spun around. He'd followed, like a cat on soft paws, and startled me. "Shit!"

"Don't swear." He frowned, then saw the cloth in my hand. His eyebrow arched up in question.

"Here, use this." I handed it to him.

He held it up. The old nightshirt hung to the floor. "It's big, but it'll do."

"Bathroom is the next door."

"Figured that out, *cher*," he called over his shoulder, as he strolled down the hall.

Cher?

I opened my mouth to comment, but the bathroom door slammed closed.

Damn, that boy tied me up. He'd be the death of me if I let him.

If he let me.

If…

I yanked one of the blankets off my bed, grabbed a pillow, and headed back to the front room. I placed them on the worn burgundy velvet sofa, then sat in a chair across from it. Next to the chair, a small side table held the book I'd been reading.

Sir Arthur Conan Doyle and that funny detective of his. I liked him. He played the violin and used disguises. I liked that he and Doctor Watson lived together. No one ever said anything about it, like it was normal.

I picked the book up, found my place, and started reading.

A few minutes later, Tommy cleared his throat. "I'm done."

I looked up and stilled, my heart coming to a complete stop.

Tommy, dressed in my night shirt, with bare feet and tousled hair, made me want to take him in my arms, kiss him until he submitted, and rip the damn shirt off him.

I marked my place, put my book on the table, and got to my feet. "Well, I'll leave you, then. Light on or off?"

"Just low is fine, if you don't mind." He went to the couch, put the pillow on one end, and spread out the blanket as I adjusted the gas lamp. When I turned around, he'd slipped under the covers.

"If it gets cold, let me know, and I'll put a log on the fire." Both the front room and the bedroom each had a small metal grated fireplace I used only on the coldest nights. Coppers don't make much money and wood ain't cheap.

"Sure." He took off his glasses and placed them on the floor next to the sofa.

I stood there, unable to move, afraid if I did, it'd be straight to the sofa and Tommy.

When he rolled over, facing the back of the sofa, it broke the spell, thank God. I swallowed, turned away, and padded down the hall to my own bed. I shut the door behind me and stared at my room.

It wasn't much to write home about, but for a copper, it wasn't bad.

I turned down my light, crawled into bed and pulled up the covers. Between Tommy and me was a forty-foot hall, one door, and all my denial.

§ § § §

In the morning, I came out of my room, the aroma of fresh coffee brewing filling the air and my nostrils. I pulled my dressing gown around me, tied it off, and headed to the kitchen.

Tommy, dressed in his clothes from last night, stood at the stove, pushing scrambled eggs around my mother's hand-me-down old cast iron frying pan. Next to it on the stove, coffee perked.

On the small kitchen table next to the wall sat two cups, ready to be used. He'd set the table for breakfast.

"You're up." He turned, picked up one of the cups and poured some coffee. "Black?" He offered it to me.

"Yeah." I took it from him. "Just sugar." I sat at the table and spooned in the four sugars. He watched, eyebrow raised. "So I like my coffee sweet. So what?"

"Did I say anything?" He worked with the eggs again, then brought the frying pan to the table and dished out the eggs between us, with my plate getting the lion's share.

"Is that all you want?" I asked.

"I'm fine. I don't eat much." He shrugged and put the pan back on the stove. Then he poured his own coffee. "Can I use your milk?" He waited at the icebox.

"Help yourself." I pointed to it with my fork, heaped with creamy eggs. "These eggs are great."

"Thanks." He poured milk into his cup, turning the black liquid the color of café au lait, then added two sugars. He sat, his hands wrapped around the cup, as if to warm them.

"Sleep okay?" I asked.

"Yes."

"Wasn't too cold?"

"No."

Okay, he wasn't much of a talker in the morning. But he could sure as hell cook. Maybe having him around for a few days wouldn't be so bad.

"I should go to the Palace. See if any of the girls or Miss Angel have returned."

"All right."

"Maybe get some clothes." He sipped the coffee, his full lips pressing against the delicate china rim. The delicate cup looked good in his hands. Better than in my big paws.

"I suppose you have to go to work?" he asked, looking at me over the cup.

Damn those eyes of his; the glasses made them look big. Beautiful. So damn blue.

"Yeah. I work the second shift. My shift starts at four this afternoon. Four to eleven tonight," I babbled. He knew that. I'd been walking that beat for years, but something about sitting here at the table, with the breakfast he'd just fixed me, that seemed too much like normal.

I wasn't normal, that much I knew. Far from it.

I suspected Tommy wasn't normal either.

But I had no proof. Neither of us did. And that was good, right?

"I better get going now."

I had nothing to say to that. I'd forced him out the back door of his home, brought him here for his protection, and now, danger past, I had no reason to keep him here.

"Okay." I shoveled the last of my food in, wiped my mouth with the napkin he'd laid out, and put down my fork. I had a few questions of my own. "You got any idea why the cops would want you?"

"No." He shook his head. "I've never been brought in before.

I'm just the piano player, not a customer. No one important."

That just gave me more to chew over.

He finished eating, stood, and swept up the plates, bringing them to the sink.

"Let me do that," I said as I rose. "You cooked. I can wash."

"Sure." He stepped aside.

I worked the pump, filled the pan with water, and put the dishes in to soak.

He cocked that damn eyebrow again. "That's what you call washing dishes?"

"Well, I soak them first." I grinned. "Easier to wash. Later."

"Right." He nodded and pushed off the counter. "Better be going." He turned and waited for me to say something.

What the hell did he want me to say?

He wasn't my slave. He wasn't a prisoner here. He wasn't even my boy.

Oh hell. My boy. Did that ever sound good. And so very bad.

"Best get to it," I said.

He frowned and left the kitchen. I could see the look of disappointment in his eyes, but fuck, what did he expect?

I went to my bedroom, threw myself on the bed, and put my arms behind my head. I heard the front door open, close, and he was gone.

He'd never said if he'd come back.

I'd never asked.

Chapter Three

How long would I wait for Tommy to return?

It was nearly two in the afternoon. I had to leave to report in by three forty-five, meet James, and get our marching orders. And I wanted to get there early enough to ask around about the raid last night.

I sat in the chair, Sherlock Holmes on my lap, gazing at the unlit fireplace.

It didn't make sense. I tried to figure it out like Holmes would have, but I couldn't. Maybe I didn't have the smarts he had. Maybe it was harder because it was real and not a story.

The Pleasure Palace shouldn't have been raided. Storyville was off-limits; had been for years. What had happened to change that? Why didn't the captain tell us about the raid? It was on our watch, after all.

And why Tommy? He couldn't have been the only one they were after. They'd gathered up nearly everyone in the place, including Miss Angel, the house madam.

Why the Palace? There were at least a couple dozen houses in Storyville. What made hers important enough to warrant a raid?

One of the gentlemen? Could be. The city's gentry included many prominent businessmen, doctors, city officials… City officials. Had one of the men been someone in power? Did someone want to embarrass him? Politicians were an oily lot.

The knock on the door jerked me back to the here and now, and the book fell to the floor as I jumped to my feet. On the other side of the frosted window, a lone figure stood, hand raised to knock again.

I pulled open the door.

Tommy.

"Did I disturb you?" he asked, lowering his hand.

"No. Just reading." I held the door open so he could get past me. He entered, carrying a small brown satchel. Inside, I figured he had some of his possessions.

"Did you get your things?" I asked. I motioned him to the sofa and took the chair again.

"Yeah. The place was still locked up, but I know how to get in." He shrugged.

"Really? Found a spare key under the mat?"

He blushed, looking at me over the rims of his glasses. "I climbed up the drainpipe on the side and crawled through a window in the kitchen. They never lock it."

"You use that to come and go often?" My turn to arch an eyebrow in his direction.

"When necessary. I've lived there my entire life." He picked at some bit of fluff on the leg of his trousers. He shifted his scuffed brown boots on the wood floor.

I stared at him. "I thought you just worked there. Hired to play."

"I was born at the Palace. My mother was Miss Angel's sister."

Knock me over with a feather. The kid's mother had been a dove.

"It's not like you think," he added quickly. "She wasn't a whore." His bottom lip quivered, but his eyes flashed ready anger at whatever he assumed I was thinking.

"I wasn't thinking that." But I was. Cops did that—put together evidence and leap to conclusions.

"I don't know who my father was." He kicked at the floor, head down.

"I don't care. I knew my father and wished I'd never met him."

Tommy's head shot up. "Oh."

Oh, hell, yeah. "Fathers aren't always what they're supposed to be, boy."

He frowned. "Why do you do that?"

"Do what?"

"Call me boy. I'm not a boy. I'm twenty-two."

Again that brave chin jut. Damn, he got to me. How could I explain it to him when I couldn't even explain it to myself?

I shrugged. "I'm older than you."

"How old?" His eyes narrowed behind the glasses.

"Thirty. Eight years older," I pointed out.

"That's not that old. Not old enough to call me a boy."

"Maybe."

He rose from the sofa and crossed the floor to me. Standing right in front of me, Tommy clenched his hands in his trousers pockets. "Do you want me to be your boy?" he whispered.

I nearly swallowed my tongue. "Hell, no!" I wanted to get out of the room, but he had me trapped in the chair.

Something flickered in his eyes, then he blinked and there was nothing. "Okay."

Do you want to be my boy? The words fought their way to my lips, but I kept them shut tight. That way led to so much danger.

He looked down at the floor. "Hey, Sherlock Holmes. I've read one of his stories." He bent down and picked up the book, just as I bent forward for it.

Our faces came close. I could feel his breath, light and rapid, against my lips.

For too long, we gazed at each other. His lips parted as he stared at my lips in an open invitation.

I had to be out of my mind. I didn't know him from Adam. He could destroy me with the police. Nancy boys weren't allowed on the force, and in Louisiana, sodomy was a crime punishable by years of hard labor.

I sat up, pulling away from him, the book in my hands.

He exhaled and straightened. Stepped away with slumped shoulders.

"So, I got some clothes and some money I'd saved from my room." He went to the satchel and picked it up.

"Did you see anyone from the Palace?"

"No. I guess they're all in jail?" He looked at me for confirmation. "I don't have enough money to make Angel's bail." He looked lost, defeated. Something inside me hated that. Made me want to make it better for him, any way I could.

I sighed. "Look, I'll check on her and the other girls when I get to work. How about that?"

His face brightened, and my heart flipped in my chest to see the beauty there.

He had to go. Sooner better than later. I was a strong man, but every man has his limits. And with Tommy, I was fast approaching mine.

"You'd do that for me?" He looked at me like I was some sort of fucking hero.

"Sure. It's no big deal." I'd planned to do it anyway, but failed to mention it to him. Being a hero ain't so bad every now and then, not if it meant getting that look from Tommy.

"Thank you!"

He plopped onto the sofa, smiling at me. I could get lost in that smile and never come up for air. But that would be drowning, right? And I'd sworn I'd never take that plunge. Not with someone who counted.

Tommy counted, and that shook me all the way through.

He really had to go.

"Do you need dinner before you leave for work?" he asked.

"No. My partner James and I eat dinner at one of the local diners. Cops eat free, you know." I grinned. "You can help yourself to anything you find in the icebox."

"Thanks."

I went to the coat rack, took down my uniform jacket and slipped into it. "Hey, before I leave, what took you so long today at the Palace?"

He blushed and pushed his hair out of his face. "My piano. I had to play it for a while."

"Right." I chuckled. "You and that damned piano."

"Hey, don't swear at my piano!" He leaped to his feet, fists clenched, prepared to defend her honor.

"Sit down, boy," I barked.

His legs gave way as if I'd cut the strings to a marionette and he landed back on the couch. I would have laughed if he weren't glaring at me to beat the band.

"Hey, I like your piano. I like the way you play that thing. Like the jazz."

Tommy relaxed, his hands opening as he rubbed them on his trousers.

I put my cap on my head. "Lock the door behind me. I don't have a spare key, so I don't leave the place unlocked. This isn't the best neighborhood. If you do leave, lock the door behind you and wait for me. My shift ends at eleven and it takes me about half an hour to get home."

Tommy nodded. "Got it. Stay put."

I opened the door and looked back. "Good boy." I shut the door before the pillow from the sofa he hurled at me struck the wall next to the door.

Chuckling, pleased as hell with myself, I trotted down the stairs.

Chapter Four

I reached the precinct at three-thirty. Not much time to check out the raid, but I knew James would cover for me if I were late. I headed over to the cells to see who was keeping residence there.

I knew the guard, so I asked him if he had the arrest sheet from last night's raid, claiming to want to check to see if I had been credited with any of the arrests.

He showed me the records for the men as I leaned over the desk, flipping through it for any names I recognized. I let out a soft, long whistle.

"Big names, huh?" the guard asked with a smirk.

"Indeed." He wasn't lying. Some of the swankest, most prestigious family names were on the list.

"Who's still here?" I wanted to know who hadn't bailed out.

"Most of the ladies." His lips twisted in thought. "One or two of the men whose wives wouldn't be caught dead bailing out their husbands from a whorehouse."

"Like who?" I ran my finger over the list of names as he looked over my shoulder.

"His Honorable Judge Matthew Brinks? I think he's still here. His wife refused to come down."

"Can I see him?"

"Going to spring him?" The guard laughed.

"Hell, no. Just want to talk to him about the raid."

He stared at me, then nodded. "Follow me."

He led me past a few cages to the holding pen. Inside, a half dozen or so men, in various states of undress and inebriation, sat on benches along the wall.

"Brinks!" he called out.

A portly man in a rumpled tuxedo looked up, hope in his pale blue eyes. "Yes? Am I free to go?"

I motioned him to come to the bars, and he rose and lumbered across the small room.

"Am I free?"

I hated to tell him no, but…

"Not yet. Just a few more questions."

"Okay." Anxious now to be let go, he was more than willing to speak with me.

"Tell me about last night. Who were you there with?"

He rattled off some of the names on the list.

"That all?"

"Of course." He looked affronted at the idea he'd lie to an officer of the law, him being a judge and all.

"Any idea why the raid? Storyville is off-limits. You know that as well as anyone, I suppose."

He blushed. "I was just as shocked as the next man when the police burst through the front door."

I got an idea. "Who wasn't shocked? Anyone look like they expected it?"

He scratched his head, then ran his hand over his face. "As a matter of fact, old Anthony Fallzone just stood there. Didn't try to make a break for it, as they say. The coppers took him out first thing."

"Fallzone, huh? Who's he?" The name wasn't familiar to me, but then I didn't rub elbows with New Orleans' finest citizens.

"Anthony? He's running against the may—" The man halted. "Say, you don't think…"

"I don't think at all. I'm just a beat copper." I'd gotten what I'd come there for, so I left.

"Hey! When am I getting out?" he yelled after me.

"Soon as your wife makes your bail," I called back.

The guard let me out, laughing as he closed the door on the judge's cries for help.

I understood now. Politicians and their games. So, how did Fallzone know about the raid? He had to have known. And the police had to have known about him or why else would they have hustled him out of the Palace?

"Let me see that list again."

The guard sighed, and dragged out the ledger. I flipped it to the second to last entry and scanned the names again.

Just as I thought. Anthony Fallzone hadn't been arrested last night.

§ § § §

"Where the hell have you been? I had to cover for you last night," James whispered to me as I took my place beside him in line. The captain was pacing back and forth in front of the first line of men, giving us a good dressing down. Luckily, James and I were in the last row and at the far end, so the cap didn't notice me arriving late.

"Thanks. I owe you."

"The captain will have your stripes, and you know that," he warned me.

I wasn't worried. Not really. Not for being late. Sure, he'd rake me over the coals, maybe give me hell for a day or so, but it would be nothing like what would happen if he ever found out I fucked men.

At last, the lecture ended and we were sent out. James and I climbed up into the wagon they used to drop the men off at their beats. We leaned over the wooden rails and watched the city go by.

New Orleans had been my home ever since my father and mother got off the steamer docked here. They'd chosen not to go to New York, but to try their luck down south.

It hadn't been a bad decision. There were lots of bars for my old man to drink in, and lots of work for my mother. Me, my three brothers and one sister had all done okay. Two brothers worked the docks, one in a restaurant, and my sis had married and was spitting out little Irish babes like she'd been born to it.

Me, I'd always wanted to be a cop. Being a detective was a dream I'd woken to once I was on the force. It meant more money and more prestige and even a big, dumb Irish like me could make the grade.

The wagon reached Basin Street, slowed, and James and I jumped off, and the men we replaced climbed up and took our places. We took a moment to straighten our uniforms, get out our batons, and check the street. Everything looked normal, but the worried looks on the faces of the maids overseeing the workers readying the houses for the evening's fun let us know something was up.

And the look of distrust when we passed…

"Feel it?" I asked James.

"No. My hands are occupied at the moment." James guffawed at his joke.

I laughed right along with him. Keeping up appearances, I suppose.

"I'm talking about the atmosphere on the street." I pointed to Miss Lavidia, who stood on her steps, wringing her hands and looking around as if expecting a paddy wagon with her name on it to turn the corner and stop at her place.

"She does look worried." James frowned, probably thinking about his little whore.

I wanted to talk over my suspicions with James, but I was afraid he'd wonder why I cared so damn much. I wasn't about to tell him, so I just put it in my back pocket and chewed on it.

Me, I was just trying to keep Tommy off my mind, but it was damned hard. Thoughts of the boy floated in and out of my head, giving my prick a workout. I needed him to get out of my house before my resolve broke.

I also needed to find out what was up with that raid. I knew it wasn't my job, not my place, but something inside me went protective over Tommy. If his home and his damned piano were being threatened, then I wanted to help.

James had crossed the street, and I'd trailed after him. He headed straight for the Pelican and Miss Lavidia.

"Good evening," he greeted her.

She jumped like a cat on a hot tin roof. "Oh! Officer Stoli. Officer O'Rourke. Good evening." She fanned her face and leaned against the front door.

"Miss Lavidia," I said. "Terrible about the Palace, wasn't it?"

"Oh, dearie, such a shame! I don't know what Miss Angel is going to do." She glanced across the street with real sorrow in her eyes. These ladies might be competing for business, but they were sisters of the heart.

I went up a couple of steps, so I could talk to her without anyone else in the street hearing. "Why the Palace? Everyone knows Storyville is protected."

"Ask your boss." She sniffed and glared at us.

"Not me!" I held up my hands in denial.

"Sure. Like I didn't see you and James rushing to help the officers." She frowned at us both with a look reserved for incorrigible boys and wayward girls.

"We rushed over there to help," James said. "I got upstairs as fast as I could to get the girls out the back."

Miss Lavidia gave him a warm smile, then turned to me, eyebrows raised.

"And you?"

I swallowed. If I took the role of copper, she'd never talk to me honestly. If I admitted to helping Tommy escape, there was James to deal with.

"I found that fool piano boy still playing. I hustled him out the back door before the coppers got him." I shrugged. "Just trying to help, that's all."

James gave me a look, and I knew I'd surprised him, but he said nothing.

"Oh, that's good. That boy is Angel's favorite. He's her nephew, you know." She nodded. "She'll appreciate that, when she gets back."

"Speaking of that, do you know when she'll return?" The faster she got back, the sooner I could get Tommy—and temptation—out of my house.

"I heard she's getting one of her benefactors to pay her bail tomorrow." She shrugged. "She'll have to gather up the girls and reopen."

"Good news, then." I doffed my cap to her and headed back down the stairs.

"Tell Miss Victoria I'm sorry I couldn't come by last night." James gave her a sheepish grin.

"Don't worry. She knew about the raid." Lavidia lit a cigarette and inhaled deeply.

"Well, good." James looked relieved.

I grabbed his arm and dragged him down the steps. "Enough mooning."

James laughed, and we continued down the street.

Time passed before he spoke. "So, you got the piano player out?"

"Yeah. Dumb kid was just sitting there. Not enough sense to run."

"You never showed up after the raid. I looked for you. Where'd you run off to?" James's voice had lowered and taken a tone I hadn't heard before. Suspicious.

"The kid didn't have a place to stay. He lives there." I jerked my thumb over my shoulder at the Palace behind us. "He had no money, nothing. I just helped him find a place to stay."

James stopped. "I've seen that kid. He's no kid." James's gaze held mine.

"So?"

"Just saying. He's a grown man. Doesn't he have friends to stay with?"

"Seems not. The Palace is his home. Most of the girls were arrested, including Miss Angel, and the place locked up. Where could he go?"

James ran his hand down his face. "Don't tell me, please don't tell me, you took him home with you?"

"Why not? It's just a few days. You heard it. He'll be out of my hair in no time." I don't know how the hell I'd let this conversation go this far.

"Max, the piano player is a faggot. Even I know that." He spit the word "faggot" out like it burned his mouth. My stomach clenched and took a hard roll, and the idea James would use that word to describe me if he knew just tore me up.

"Is he?" I shrugged, like it didn't mean a thing to me.

"You know what people will say about you if anyone finds out he's staying with you?" James huffed out a breath. "You can't be that stupid."

"Just because I let a down-on-his-luck guy spend a few nights at my place doesn't mean I'm a nancy." I gave him a glare back that I hoped would shut him up. "Besides, like Lavidia said, the Palace will be open tomorrow, and he can go home then. And do I look like a nancy to you?" I squared off to him, big fists on hips, stance spread.

He looked me up and down, as if seeing me for the first time. My wide shoulders, broken nose, close-cropped dark hair, my large mitts. If anything, I looked like a prizefighter.

"Well..." James seemed to accept that for now.

Thank God.

For the rest of the shift, something was just off between James and me. I knew we were still partners, but I worried that if I needed him, James might not be there for me.

Chapter Five

When the shift was over, James headed to see Miss Victoria, and I headed home. The night was chilly; November's bite in the air. I needed time to think, so I walked through the Vieux Carre to the Marigny.

For a while, I stood outside my own house, both dreading and anticipating going inside. At what I'd find there. At Tommy, waiting for me.

Tried to think about what it would be like to come home to him every night.

I couldn't. Men like us didn't do that. We didn't have lives like that. Have homes. Our lives were spent hiding, dodging shadows, looking over our shoulders or hiding behind the skirts of some woman we'd conned into marrying us.

I would never do that to a woman. First off, I don't want to live with one, much less marry one. I didn't have any inclination to have a bunch of brats running around either. I left that to my brothers and sisters.

So, whatever cozy little scene of domesticity awaited me tonight, it was an illusion. I squared that in my head and went up the steps, unlocked the door and went inside.

Tommy lay on the couch, under the blanket, reading one of my books. He looked up, grabbed his glasses off the side table, and put them on. "Hey!" He sat up, the book tossed to the side.

"Hey. Everything okay?" He wore the same nightshirt I'd given him last night. I wondered if it would smell like him after he left. Decided if it did, never to wash it.

I'm a fucking idiot.

"Fine. Nothing happened. Did you see my Aunt Angel?" He leaned forward, eyes bright and hopeful.

"I didn't have time to see her, but she's going to make bail tomorrow."

He exhaled. "That's good."

"Right. So you can leave." I took off my jacket and hung it up with my cap.

Tommy looked at me like I'd kicked a kitten. "Sure. If that's what you want."

If that's what I want? Fuck. What did I want? *No. Hell, no.* I'm not admitting that, not even to myself.

"Figured you'd want to get back to the Palace. To your piano. Not hang out here with a cop." *With a man like me.*

Tommy looked down at his hands, with their long, tapering fingers. He had strong corded forearms, for a man of his youth and size.

"You're not so bad," he got out, his throat sounding all tight and closed off.

What I wanted…those hands on me. On my face, my back, my cock.

I cleared my throat. It had gone tight also, right along with my trousers. I needed to get out of there, fast, before I did something I'd regret.

"I'm beat. 'Night." I turned away and headed down the hall. I stopped in the kitchen for a glass of water. Tommy didn't follow, thank God. I leaned against the kitchen table as I drained the glass, trying not to think about fucking him as he bent over the table.

My fantasies were escaping my bedroom now. This thing with Tommy was getting out of control fast. I put the dish down and went to my room. Stripped down, hung up my uniform, turned down the lamp, and in my drawers, climbed under the covers.

Tomorrow Tommy would leave…and my life could go back to the way it was—lonely. But safe.

So, so, very safe.

And that's what I wanted. Above all. My job as a good cop.

§ § § §

I have no idea what time it was when my door opened, but I came out of the bed like I'd heard the clanging of a fire wagon.

"What the fuck?" I staggered, unsteady on my feet.

Tommy stood in the doorway. In the faint light of my gas lamp, I could just make him out. I fell back to sit on the bed and ran my hands through my hair, then over my eyes, trying to clear my head and settle my racing heart.

He didn't say a word. I looked up. "What's wrong?" My gut tightened at the thought Tommy needed me.

"I'm not in your bed." His voice floated on the air, hidden in the dark, but it still found me. Dumbfounded.

I opened my mouth, but he'd already started toward me. Whatever I was going to say froze somewhere between my throat and my mouth as I watched him. Halfway to me, he shrugged off the too-big nightshirt and stepped out of it, leaving it in a heap on the floor.

I didn't move, afraid to break the spell or wake from this dream. Because this had to be a dream. One of my fantasies…the ones I'd been having every night since I first saw Tommy. The ones I'd been pleasuring myself to for almost two damn years.

He stopped right in front of me.

Fantasy? Dream?

I reached out and captured his hips in my hands. Real. Flesh and blood. Warm skin, soft to the touch. *Oh, fuck*. I closed my eyes and struggled for control.

Tommy crawled onto my lap, and I let him. He knelt, his knees on the bed on either side of my legs, his ass on my thighs, and his cock, stiff and proud, dragging over my belly. My own cock tented my drawers and my mouth went bone-dust dry.

"Max?" His soft voice held so much question. I didn't have the answers to any of them. Not in my mind. But my body? It had all the right answers.

"Shut up, boy." I slid my hand up his back to cup his head and drew him to me. He buried his face in the crook of my neck and slipped his arms around my neck. Our bodies pressed against each other, trapping his cock between us, and my cock, well, somewhere next to it.

"I've only ever wanted to be your boy," he admitted, muffled against my shoulder.

"I said shut up." I couldn't take it, not the stuff he was saying. Not the hope in his voice, and I sure as hell couldn't bear to see what he held in his gaze.

Instead, I pulled his head up, held it still and kissed him. His lips, plump and soft, pressed against mine and then, like heaven's gates, opened to let this sinner in.

I explored his mouth with my tongue, as he moaned, his fingers gripping my back, digging into my flesh. That sound shot straight to my cock, and I pushed my drawers down to free it.

Both our pricks danced, until I caught them with my hand and stroked them.

Tommy shuddered, gasped, breaking our kiss. "Oh God!" His back arched as he thrust against me, as I took control.

I stroked again and again, my rough hand sliding over his cock and mine, servicing us and spreading the leaking fluid over both. He threw his head back and cried out, something garbled and incoherent, and I latched onto his throat, biting and sucking, all pretense of control gone.

He was my boy, and I would have him.

"Max! Oh, Max!" It was a sob now, as he chanted my name. I licked up his throat, nipped his ear, pulling it, then recapturing his mouth.

"I can't stop it—" he cried and spilled over my hand, his chest, my belly. He was barely a man, after all.

I gave his cock a few gentle strokes and let it go, then continued to work my shaft, hard and aching. As the elder of us, the more experienced from what I could tell, I needed just a bit more.

Tommy pushed away from me. "Wait. Let me." He slid off my legs to the floor, pushing my thighs apart and kneeling in front of me. He took over my pumping, his gaze feverish and dark.

I wrapped my hand around the back of his head, burying my fingers in his mop of blond hair. "Suck me, boy."

He obeyed. I'm not sure what I'd have done if he hadn't, but thank God, I didn't have to find out. He opened his mouth and gave the head of my cock a few tentative licks, tasting me like he might not like the flavor. And then it hit me—he'd never done this before.

The boy lived in a whorehouse and he'd never…

Well, that slowed me down, knocked the wind right outta my sails. How the hell could I fuck him if he'd never been fucked before? If I had doubts before, this one took first place. Was I corrupting him? Leading him down a path that in all rights, I should be protecting him from?

"Tommy, wait." I pulled him off, and he sat back on his heels, looking up at me, blinking as if trying to focus his vision on me.

"What's wrong? What did I do?"

"You've never done it, have you? Been with another man?"

He looked down at the floor, didn't answer.

"Tommy." My tone demanded an answer.

"No." He shook his head, still not looking up at me.

I sighed.

"I'm not a kid," he yelled. His fists clenched on his thighs and his shoulders straightened. "I know what I want."

"Do you?" If I left him alone, maybe he'd fall for some girl. One of the girls at the Palace, or one of the other bordellos. Maybe have a normal life.

"I want you." He looked up into my eyes, chin up, defiant, sure.

"It's not too late for you. You can still—"

"What? Be 'normal'?" He stood and paced to the other side of the bedroom. "Get married? Have kids?" He crossed his arms over his chest, hugging himself. "I don't want that life."

"But this life…this life isn't easy. We can't have a life like you want."

"How do you know what I want?" he shot back. "You don't even know me."

"Good point." I stood and tucked my waning prick back into my drawers. "You don't know me. I don't know you. Now, go back to bed."

He started toward me, but I held out a hand. "The couch."

His bottom lip trembled. "Fuck you!" He bolted out of the room and down the hall.

"Fuck me is right," I muttered as I sat on the bed again.

Chapter Six

The next morning, I slept late. Part of me hoped Tommy had left; the other part hoped he'd still be here. But after a while, the aroma of freshly perked coffee snaked its way into my room. I rolled over, exhaled, and knew I had to get up and face Tommy.

After I dressed, I walked to the kitchen, where Tommy sat at the table. "I made breakfast." He avoided my gaze, but that was just as well for me. I didn't want to see the hurt in his eyes.

"Thanks." I took a plate and served myself from the skillet—eggs and some sausage, all mixed together—and then sat.

"I'm packed." Tommy licked his lips.

"All right." I nodded and took a bite, chewing slowly to give me time to think of something to say to make this better.

There wasn't anything to make this better. I wanted him. He wanted me. It was impossible. I'd known it all along, knew it two years ago when I first saw him, and now it was Tommy's turn to know it.

He rose and placed his plate in the sink, finished his coffee, and put the cup there, too. "I'll be going back to the Palace. I hope my aunt's out of jail, but if she's not, I'm going to get the place cleaned up. It was a mess from the raid. She'll want to reopen as soon as she can."

"Sure. That'll be nice." I didn't know what else to tell him. Well, nothing I could say that wouldn't give him hope. He needed to leave. I needed him gone, more than I needed him.

He opened his mouth and then closed it. Then opened it and said, "I'm not giving up on us, Max." He pushed off the counter and left the room.

What the hell was that supposed to mean?

I sat there, listening to him move around the living room. The front door opened, closed and he was gone.

I couldn't breathe. All the air in my chest had gone, sucked out when he left, and it scared the hell outta me. He was really gone, and I couldn't breathe without him. What the hell?

I got to my feet and staggered to my room, my chest heaving, gulping for air like a fish on a bank. I bent over, hands on my knees, sucking in air at last. My breathing calmed and my heart slowed its hammering.

I'd survive. Just like I had been my entire life. Just keep it hidden, keep it out of the limelight, and everything would be good.

My life would be just as I'd planned it. I'd still be a cop, maybe make detective next year. I'd have everything I'd ever wanted.

Except Tommy.

§ § § §

I got to the station house an hour early, just to do some more snooping around. Despite giving Tommy up, I wasn't going to stop looking out for him. He was still my boy, I suppose, deep down in my heart.

My captain had ordered the raid, ordered Tommy be taken, so maybe that's where I should start asking questions. Except queries like that could put an end to my career as a copper, and I could forget making detective.

All the captain's orders came through our sergeant and I knew just the way to ask my questions of him.

I found him in the day room at his desk.

"Hey, Sergeant, got a minute?" I strolled over, making my walk as much like James' cocky stride as possible.

Sergeant Jan Howe looked up at me. "What's up?" He grinned at me. Other coppers could say what they will about Sarge, but he's a stand-up guy.

"About that raid on the Palace… James and me were just wondering why you didn't let us in on it." I looked as sheepish as possible. "You're not upset with us, are you? Did we do something wrong?"

"Hell, no!" He leaned back in his chair and it creaked with old age and his weight. Sarge was not a small man. In fact, the big Norwegian made me look small. "Look, I'll tell you the truth. We didn't get the orders until about thirty minutes before I sent the wagon out. No time to contact you boys." He shrugged. "It didn't mean a thing."

"Well, good. It's just that James and me, we got orders not to do any arrests in Storyville and then here's this raid happening, and we don't know shit about it, pardon my French, and we got to worrying if we'd missed something." I shifted from one foot to the other, my cap in my hands.

"Hey, all I know is the captain got a call on the telephone, and next thing I knew, I was ordering out the wagon." He shrugged.

"Maybe the Palace didn't pay?" I laughed and winked.

"More like he was just doing what he'd been told to do."

"Someone told the cap'n what to do?" I scoffed. "Who could do that?"

Howe looked up at me again. "If you want to make detective, O'Rourke, you'd better learn the ropes. The brass takes their orders from higher up and no questions asked."

"Got it!" I nodded and put my hat back on my head. "It's almost shift change. Thanks, Sarge."

He went back to work as I walked off. Only some of my questions had been answered, but I'm sure I kept Sarge from wondering why I asked. So, the call came from above the brass of the force and that left only a few places that held that sort of power—city hall, the Catholic church or the new rising organization, the Brothers of Italy.

Anthony Fallzone, although Italian, wasn't a priest.

I decided to look into him a little closer. I knew, though, it'd have to be on my own time. But where to start? How would I find out about him? I went through my list of contacts, people I could go to in the neighborhood I lived in, and in Storyville, for answers.

Then it hit me. My partner was Italian.

I hurried off to the squad room, got in line with the others, next to James and we listened to Sarge give our orders for the night. When the men broke up and headed out, James and me went along to the wagon.

James leaned on the rails, looking at the city go by.

"Hey, you know a guy named Anthony Fallzone?" I asked, keeping my voice low.

He straightened and turned to me, his hands clutching the wooden rail. His knuckles were white. I looked up at him, and he'd gone a shade paler.

"Why are you asking about him?" James licked his lips.

"Just a name I heard." I shrugged. "What's up with him?" I gave him the once-over. "You looked like you seen a ghost."

James swallowed and leaned down again. I followed suit. What James was going to say he didn't want anyone hearing?

"He's big in the Brothers." James lowered his voice to a whisper. "He's not someone you want to mix it up with, Max. Whatever you heard, forget it."

I took that in. "So, why would he order the raid on the Palace?"

James jerked. "He did? You sure?" he hissed.

I nodded.

He wiped his hand over his face. "Word is, he's gonna run for mayor."

Okay, he wanted to be mayor. What did raiding a whorehouse have to do with that? He'd close them down after he got to be mayor, right? Take the credit for cleaning up the city? Why before?

"What do you know about him?"

James shrugged. "He's rich. Made his money in the family funeral business. I heard his family was important back in Italy." Another shrug. "He's married. Got kids. Typical wop." James gave me a grin.

"Yeah, typical." I let it drop, and James looked relived.

So what did a man like Fallzone have to do with the Palace? And why did he want Tommy?

We reached our stop and jumped out of the wagon.

Once we'd straightened our uniforms, James got out his baton, I put on my cap, and we began this night's beat.

Once again, I'd walk past the Palace, hear Tommy playing his piano, and know I'd never have him.

Chapter Seven

A week went by. One long, lonely week. Every time we walked by the Palace, I'd hear Tommy playing his piano, only every song he played was sad. Like someone had died. And that just killed me.

It only got me thinking more about him and his connection to the Palace. How did that link to Fallzone? My brain went in circles, but one thing never led to another and I was back where I started, with nothing to go on.

Business was back to usual in Storyville.

Articles appeared in the *Picayune* about a group of righteous women demanding the mayor close the district, but I'd seen those before. Nothing ever came of it.

The election neared.

I opened the Sunday paper over breakfast and slapped my hand down.

Anthony Fallzone had declared his intention to run for mayor. His picture, bold as day, was on the back page of the first section of the newspaper, a big grin on his face. I stared at him.

He looked like a lot of men—average. Average looks, average build. He didn't look Italian. He wasn't dark, but his hair was, at least in the photograph. He wore glasses and a dark suit and white gloves, like he was all dressed up for the opera.

I tore the page out and threw the rest of the paper away in the trashcan. Then I read the article. Anthony Fallzone, son of prosperous business owners, family man, good Catholic; all the same things said of any of the mayor's opponents. Not that there were a lot of them, but there were a few.

The mayor was liked, but that didn't mean everyone liked him.

Nothing in the article quoted Fallzone saying he was going to close Storyville.

So I was back to square one.

Longing for a man I couldn't have. Trying to protect him from who the hell knew what.

Trying to be a good copper.

So many things at odds, it was a wonder I didn't just tear in two.

My heart sure felt like it.

Time to get ready for work. I pushed Tommy to the back of my mind and went through the motions.

§ § § §

James and I had done our third round when the faint clanging of a fire wagon's bell got our attention. We froze, sniffing the wind, trying to tell if it was in our district or on the other side of Rampart Street in the Vieux Carre.

Fire scared the crap outta me. It hadn't been that long since most of Chicago had burned to the ground, and New Orleans would be no different.

James had grabbed my arm, squeezing it hard. "What do you think?"

I inhaled. The scent of smoke hit my nostrils, making them itch. I sneezed.

"It's close."

Both of us scanned the tops of the buildings around us, looking for telltale signs of fire. The sky lit with orange and smoke darker than the night sky.

James pointed. "There!" Above the housetops, the sky glowed.

The clanging got louder, and people spilled onto the street. The crowd's noise was getting as loud as the bell. People started to move toward the intersection, heading to watch.

If they were smart, they'd head in the other direction.

James and I were coppers, so we took off toward the fire. We knew they'd need every man they could get to fight it, keep it from taking the entire city.

We made it to the corner, turned and dashed down the block. The fire wagon, its horses' hooves skittering on the cobblestones, sending sparks flying, rounded the corner and headed down Basin Street.

Please, not the Palace. Please.

We skidded around the corner. In the middle of the block, flames burst from the windows on the ground floor. Of the Palace.

I froze, my legs unwilling to move. James raced ahead of me.

Tommy.

And the next breath, I was off, running to catch up. Running to find James. Running to find Tommy.

We reached the building. People were pouring out the front door, jumping out of the second-floor windows. Screams and the crackle of the fire, the fire bell clanging, the forming crowd across the street, all the noise I heard, but not the sound I searched for—Tommy's piano.

Miss Angel stood, arms wrapped around one of the girls, across the street. I ran to her.

"Where's Tommy?"

She sobbed. "Inside."

I turned back to look at the house. The front door stood open. The firemen were pumping the levers on the wagon, with some bystanders helping. A few of them stood on the sidewalk, holding the hose.

A bucket brigade started. I ran to the first man with a bucket of water, grabbed it, and bounded up the steps.

"Tommy!" The smoke was thick, gray, and filling the tall first floor, covering the ceiling.

"Tommy!" I held the bucket, ready to douse him if I needed to, as I moved down the hallway.

A huge black shape came out down the hall. I staggered back, out of its way.

The piano.

"Tommy!" I covered my mouth and nose with a handkerchief.

"Max!" I'd never been so relieved to hear my name, but I still didn't see him.

"What are you doing? Let's get outta here!" The piano passed me, and I grabbed Tommy.

"Help me!"

"What the hell do you think I'm doing?" I shook him with one hand, then dumped the bucket over his head.

"Hey!" Tommy glared at me through the smoke. He shook me off and pushed the piano again. "Forget me…push!"

I fell in behind him, outta my mind, and pushed that goddamned piano down the rest of the hall, and out the front door. Tommy ran around to the front to ease it down the steps, but I'd had about enough of it. Tommy had risked his life for an old, beat-up piano.

I was going to kill him when I got my hands on him.

I shoved hard and it went down, keys banging as it thumped down each step to the banquette. Tommy leaned on it, sucking in air, as the firemen worked the hoses. Someone shouted for him to get out of the way.

I helped him push the thing to the side, down the block, out of harm's way.

Miss Angel appeared at his side, and he threw his arms around her. "Are you all right?"

She nodded, her face soot-streaked.

"What happened?" I took her arm and brought her around to

me.

"Someone threw something in the window. It hit the floor and whoosh"—she threw her hands up in the air—"fire everywhere!"

I'd never seen one before, but I'd heard. A bottle filled with kerosene, most likely, with a rag stuffed in the mouth. Light it and toss. Someone had tried to burn the place down, with everyone inside.

"It landed right by the piano." Tommy grabbed my hand and led me to the other side of the piano. I stared at the charred wooden cabinet. "I had enough time to get the flames out, then push it out of the room."

"You should've just gotten out, boy." I growled at him, but he just grinned at me.

"Oh, Tommy, you could've been killed!" His aunt threw herself at him again, sobbing. "Why did you have to save that old piano?"

Why, indeed? I waited for the answer, even if she didn't.

"It belonged to my mother." Tommy looked at me. "It's the only thing I have of her..." He ran his hand over the keys. "She loved music. And this."

I slumped against the building, my legs wobbling. "Shit, boy, I nearly lost you." I ran my hands over my face.

"Oh, Max." He laughed, and I got lost in that smile, those eyes. "You'll never lose me."

Chapter Eight

I didn't have much time to pull myself together. James rushed over to me. "Good. You got the kid out. Now, let's help with the fire. They need every man they can get on the bucket line."

I followed him, with Tommy right behind me. "Where are you going?" I threw over my shoulder.

"To help." He gave me a hard glare, and I knew not to argue. It was his home, in the first place. Second, he was grown enough to help. Even a young boy could fill and carry a bucket.

James, Tommy, and I got into the line, passing the buckets of water along, until the firemen at the end of the line took it, raced into the building and came back out, bucket empty.

The heat from the fire nearly scorched us and soot coated our bodies. I ignored all that, focusing on the knowledge taking shape in my brain.

Someone had tried to kill Tommy.

§ § § §

Hours later, nothing was left of the house but the brick chimneys, the front steps and the masonry piers that supported the building above the ground.

Miss Angel had left, taken away by a few of her girls. She'd been stoic through it all, but at the end, when there was nothing left but smoking rubble, she broke down and sobbed.

Tommy watched her go, then he turned to me and shrugged. I knew he was asking, What now?

He climbed up on his piano and sat, chin in his hands, elbows on his knees, waiting for me as I finished up with James and the new coppers who'd come on duty.

I had no idea what to do with Tommy or his piano. James stared at him, shook his head, then he slapped me on the back. "I'll call for a wagon and help you get it loaded."

I nodded.

We both knew what I had to do. Or rather, what I was going to do. I didn't have to do anything but walk away. Sometime, during the fire, the smoke, and the buckets, James realized I wasn't going to do that—walk away from Tommy.

That should have made me feel better, but it scared the hell outta me. I only hoped James figured it was friendship, and I couldn't not help a friend, right? Right?

He returned with a horse and wagon. It took him, me, Tommy and a couple of the firemen still there to load the piano into the back of the wagon and tie it down. Then Tommy climbed in the back with it, and I got up front with the driver and waved James goodbye.

"See you tomorrow at roll call," he shouted at me. The smirk on his face told me everything. If he didn't know, he suspected. I think I died a little inside, in my gut, at the worry that ate at me. James could destroy me with a word in our captain's ear.

I'd just have to trust him. Or make my denial and explanation believable.

I looked over my shoulder at Tommy. He'd wrapped his arms around the piano as if he could hold it in place. More like he was back there telling it he'd never leave it.

Him and that damned piano.

How was I ever going to get them outta my life?

By the time we reached home, the sun was coming up and I knew I was lying to myself. I wanted Tommy and that old piano in my life for a long, long time.

The driver helped us unload it, then push it to the front steps of my little house. We got it up the stairs and into the front room without too much damage to ourselves.

I gave the driver two silver dollars. He grinned at them and took off. I shut the front door and turned, only to find Tommy moving the furniture.

"What the hell are you doing?"

"Making room for my piano." He put down the side table he carried and then maneuvered the piano into place against the wall. "Looks good here." He brushed off his hands and stood back. "'Course, I need a bench or a chair to sit on."

I collapsed in my chair and ran my hands through my hair. This kid was going to kill me.

He laughed and crawled into my lap. "Thanks, Max." He kissed my cheek, then wiped it off with the arm of his shirt. Soot covered us both. We needed a bath.

"For?" I knew what, but just wanted to hear him say it.

"For letting me bring my piano home."

"Home?" I gave him a cocked eyebrow and a hard glare.

"Home." He nodded. He wore this goofy expression, sort of proud and shy and hungry, all rolled into one.

"Let's get cleaned up." I rose, nearly dumping him on the floor, but he found his feet and stood.

"You have enough hot water?" he asked, already stripping off his vest and shirt. He dumped them on the floor.

"Wait a minute!" I gathered up his clothes. "Soot'll get everywhere. Go to the bathroom and take off the rest there."

He nodded and took off down the hall. I heard the water run in the bathtub. "Don't use all the hot water. Leave me some!"

He laughed and something inside my chest eased a bit.

"Where's the soap? Oh, never mind. Found it," he called.

I leaned in the doorway of the bathroom. His shoes, pants, drawers, and socks sat in a pile on the black-and-white tiled floor. With his back to me, he climbed into the bathtub, lowered himself down, and leaned back with a sigh. Had to admit, it was a fine sight to see.

I gave him a good look as I leaned over the tub to turn off the water at the spigot. "Get clean. Don't lollygag, boy." He looked even finer in the full light from the lamp, despite the soot.

He lathered up a washrag and began to clean up.

"You can get out of your dirty clothes, Max." He winked at me as he rubbed the cloth over his chest.

I grew up with two brothers. Getting naked in front of another man, well, it's practically natural for me. But stripping down in front of Tommy, well, it sort of made me nervous. What if he didn't like what he saw? Regretted being here?

But I had to get clean at some point. Might as well be now. My uniform would need a cleaning, but that could wait until later. I'd take it to the laundry a few blocks away, and let them wash and iron it for me. It'd cost, but I only had one.

So I took off my jacket, my shirt, trousers, shoes and socks, and stood there in my drawers and undershirt, watching him wash and rinse his hair.

Tommy finished his bath, but the water was black. He let it out, then filled it with fresh water, and quickly washed again.

"Hurry up. It's cold."

"Hold your horses. I'm not clean." This time the water was gray, and he pulled the plug and let the water out. Then he stood, naked as the day he was born, and reached for a towel. I watched as he dried off, rubbing that towel over his chest, back, legs, and feet. Even his half-hard cock and balls got a rub. Wrapping the towel around his waist, he got out of the tub.

"Your turn."

"There better be hot water left," I grumbled as I yanked my undershirt over my head and pushed my drawers down. Naked, I leaned over the tub, replaced the plug and started the water. "You're lucky. It's still hot."

He laughed as he leaned against the door. "I could look at you all day and all night." He shook his head, as if he couldn't believe what he saw.

I looked down. Most of the soot was on my clothes, but even so, it had worked its way through to my skin. I didn't wait for the tub to fill, but got in and settled down, leaning back against the porcelain coated iron.

I exhaled, letting the tension gathered in my muscles escape. Exhausted. I needed to sleep because I had to report for duty at four.

"Let me."

I opened my eyes and Tommy had knelt next to the tub. He had the washcloth and the bar of soap and was working up a lather.

"What?"

"Let me wash you. You look beat." He picked up my arm and started to scrub.

"Don't be silly. I'm a grown man. I can bathe myself." I tried to pull away, but the strength of Tommy's grip surprised me.

"Relax. Max, I'm your boy. Let me do this for you."

How could I deny him when he looked at me that way?

I sighed and sat back.

Eyes closed, I let him wash me. Head to toe, and back again. Then he washed my hair and rinsed it. All the while, his hands and that cloth soothed me like I hadn't been soothed…well, ever. My muscles felt like jelly and I wondered how I'd ever get out of the tub.

At some point, I might have fallen asleep. When I realized he'd let the water out and was refilling the tub, I sat up.

"Just let me rinse you off one last time." He leaned over and shut off the water. Something inside me rose up, along with my cock. He'd cared for me, treated me better than any one had, and I wanted to thank him.

I grabbed him behind the neck and pulled him into the tub. Water splashed, and he cried out, but then he stopped struggling and just sort of sank into me. Like he belonged there. In my arms.

I couldn't fight it anymore. I was tired of it; tired of struggling against him, against us, against everything I wanted with him.

I ran my hands over his chest, and he wiggled, like a puppy, dragging his ass over my cock. The friction and the water just set me off, getting me hard. I wrapped my arms around his chest.

"Keep still!"

He halted, his body tense. I pushed his head back against my shoulder, ran my other hand down his chest, belly, over that fine blond hair around his cock, then had him in my hand.

Tommy whimpered.

Just that sound would undo me. Needy. Hungry for what I could give him. What only I could give him.

I stroked him, and he groaned, arching against my body, head back just far enough and close enough for me to turn my head and take his mouth. I bullied my way in with my tongue. Tommy moaned, and reached up to bury his fingers in my hair, holding us together as I tasted him.

I knew right then, I'd do anything for him.

And I'd kill anyone who tried to hurt him.

Chapter Nine

I slid my hand up and down along the fine length of his cock, and he bucked. Water splashed over the sides of the tub, and I figured, if we were going to become more involved, we needed to move to the bed.

As much as I hated to, I let him go and broke the kiss. He whimpered and pouted at me.

"Bed."

His eyes widened and he scampered out of the tub, grabbed the towel and dried off. I took my time, letting the desire and the need for him build in my balls. He handed me the towel, and I dried off, my erection pointing its way to him, like the needle of a compass. He was my true north.

He leaned against the sink, watching, his gaze on my cock, and when he licked his lips, I nearly exploded. Damn, he made me crazy.

I didn't trust myself to speak, so I gave a jerk of my head toward the bedroom, and he bolted. As if I would chase him. His laughter floated down the hallway as I made my way to the back of the house.

I took my time, gathering my thoughts and my resolve. He was a virgin. I'd need to go slow, take it easy, be careful not to hurt him. But my body wanted fast and hard. For now, I couldn't have that. I'd have to slow it down. Take my time with him.

The idea of lingering over Tommy's body took hold in my head, and I smiled.

When I finally made it to the bedroom, Tommy lay on the bed, naked, spread out for me like Sunday dinner. And I was starving.

"God, Max," Tommy gasped, "what are you going to do to me?"

For a moment, fear flitted across his face, then his hunger returned. Hunger for me. God, I loved that about him. He wanted me as much as I wanted him. He wasn't like the boy-whores on Rampart Street, with their fake smiles and moaning, acting like they wanted you.

Tommy really wanted me.

Something inside me went all soft and warm. My cock went rock hard. Tommy's gaze never left mine as I approached him.

"You're mine, boy." I took his foot and squeezed it, not hard, but enough to let him know I was there.

"Yours." He nodded.

I stroked his leg, running my hand up it as I climbed onto the bed. On all fours I stalked him, until I crouched over him. His cock stood against his belly; a drop or two of liquid leaked onto his stomach. I bent down and licked it off, letting the taste of it burst in my mouth.

Tommy moaned. He clutched the blanket in his fists as he threw his head back.

I licked up the length of him and it warmed my tongue. The boy was on fire, his skin radiating heat. I inhaled, breathing deeply his scent. This was something I'd never done before—smell a man. His cock and balls, the hair around them, the way his skin smelled, slightly sweaty, but clean and fresh.

Tommy was mine, and I could take all the time I wanted with him. Smell him. Touch him. Lick and bite him, all to my heart's content.

And he could do the same to me. Like a real lover. Until that moment, I'm not sure I realized how much I'd longed for a lover. Someone to do to me all the things I wanted, dreamed, fantasized someone would do to me. Someone like Tommy. He'd been my fantasy lover for two years and now, my dreams were coming true.

"Let me." He reached for me, but I shook my head.

"No. I've waited for this for a long time." I lowered my head and inhaled again, then gathered his cock into my mouth and just held him.

Tommy groaned and bucked up, trying to get more of himself in my mouth. I wanted to take my time, though, so I pushed him back down, pinning him to the bed with my hand.

I licked him, running my tongue over his cock, around the rim of his head, teased the slit a bit, then sucked him back down again. Drops of pre-cum burst on my tongue as I savored him. He drove me nuts, the way he tasted. All Tommy. All mine.

"Please, Max," he begged. "Fuck me."

My cock hurt, it was so hard. Ached to be inside him. To be the first to take him. Me and no one else. Ever. I growled at the thought of another man touching him.

I pushed his legs farther apart, gave his balls a light squeeze, then stroked down the soft part between his balls and hole. All the time, Tommy was whimpering and moaning, his head thrashing as if I was killing him.

"Okay?"

"God, yes! Touch me, Max. Fuck me. I want to feel your cock inside me. Where it belongs."

Hell, my boy could talk dirty. And I loved it.

"Don't worry, boy. I'm going to give you everything you need." And I swore it. Whatever Tommy needed, I'd get it for him.

I sucked my finger, then pushed it against his hole. It was tight, pink, and all twisted like a closed rosebud. I massaged all around it, coaxing it to open for me. Tommy spread his legs wider, pushing his heels into the bed, struggling to get my finger inside.

I pushed again, and the tip of my finger slipped in. Tommy caught his breath, held it, and nodded at me. "More."

Another little press, and I was in to the first knuckle. My boy gasped and pushed down hard, and my finger slid in deeper.

"I said, fuck me!" He frowned.

"Can't get enough, heh?" I chuckled. My boy wanted it bad.

"No. Not until your cock is in me. Stop teasing me, Max." There was that pretty pout again.

"I'm not teasing. I'm taking care. Don't want to hurt you." I grabbed my cock with my free hand and showed it to him. "This has to go inside, boy. I could split you open if you're not ready for me."

He glanced from my prick to my eyes and nodded. "I just want you so bad…"

"I know. I know. Now let me relax you, ease into you."

He licked his lips. "Okay, Max." I could see the trust in his eyes. He'd let me do anything to him, even something that might hurt him badly, but he trusted me not to cause him pain.

I wanted to die for him, right then and there. If you want to call that love, then I guess that's what I felt for him because I'd never felt it for anyone else.

I worked my finger in and pulled it out, then back in. I finger fucked him for a few minutes, adding a finger, then working the two together. My fingers are thick, and the two of them…well, they're pretty damn close to the girth of my cock, but I added another just in case.

I didn't want Tommy to feel anything but good. No pain. Nothing to scare him, to stop him from letting me do this to him again.

But all this was making me crazy with want for him. My cock leaked and my balls ached. If I didn't get inside him soon, I was going to come. I wanted to come inside him, with him all around me. Feel his heat. His heartbeat. His orgasm.

I pulled out my fingers and jerked open the drawer of my bed table. I grabbed the bottle of oil I kept there, and poured some over my cock, then spread it with my hand. Just the touch of flesh on flesh had me ready to spill.

I lined up the head of my cock with Tommy's hole and pressed in. The head popped in, and Tommy cried out.

"Did I hurt you?"

"No!" He panted. "It's good. So good. It feels good and hurts good. More. I need more." He'd pushed up on his elbows to watch. I met his gaze and saw the hunger still there.

I couldn't help myself. I shifted forward, caught his mouth with mine and shoved deeper inside him. I swallowed his cry as I settled all the way in. He wrapped his arms around my neck and held on.

"Fuck me," he whispered.

I lowered him down and he wrapped his legs around my waist. I took my first stroke, in and out, and he closed his eyes and sighed.

"So good."

"It is. Damn, boy, I love being inside you." I thrust again, and again, and fought to keep it slow and easy, but my body wanted hard and fast.

Seemed Tommy did, too. "Harder. Want to feel you slam into me."

Dirty boy. Thank God.

I gave him what we both wanted, hard and fast. I held his hips and pistoned into him, my hips snapping, my cock reaming him. Tommy was with me all the way. He met my thrusts and opened even wider and deeper, as if our bodies were made for each other.

My end built, my balls pulled tight and I knew it'd be soon, so I angled upward and raked my cock over his button.

"Oh God! God! What the hell was that?" he cried out.

I smirked. "Like it?"

"God, yes! Do it again." He grabbed at my hair and pulled it. "It's like getting shocked."

So I hit it again, and he started trembling. "Gonna come."

"Yeah, come for me. I want to feel you."

He reached for his cock.

"That's it. Touch your prick."

Tommy stroked himself, maybe about two times, then he threw his head back, and shouted my name. White ribbons shot out of his cock and covered his chest.

Inside him, his body squeezed my prick, locking it deep inside and setting me off.

I came, shooting inside him, bathing him with my semen, marking him on the inside as mine. I shuddered and fell on top of Tommy. He wrapped his arms around me and held me tight as we both came down from our pleasure.

His legs were still wrapped around my waist, my cock was still inside him, and I pulled the blanket over us. All I wanted, I had right here and now.

Tommy in my bed. Warm and sated.

"Sleep," I ordered. I lifted up to see his face, but Tommy had already passed out.

I smiled, shifted enough to get my weight off him, and my cock slipped free. I gathered Tommy into my arms, wrapping my body around his, protecting him, and sighed.

No one would take this from me. I'd never let anyone take Tommy. Ever.

Tommy slept, while I wondered why and who wanted him dead.

Chapter Ten

I slept for a while, but after I woke, instead of taking advantage of Tommy in my bed, I got out, careful not to wake him. I had to get my uniform cleaned and ironed in time for my shift. I dressed, wrote a quick note to Tommy and put it on the kitchen table, then left.

While the laundry had my uniform, I went back to the Palace. I needed to talk to Miss Angel. Being Tommy's aunt, I figured she'd be my best bet to find out what was going on.

The street smelled of smoke, and in the light of day, the burned-out house looked forlorn. The houses on either side had only been singed, lucky for them. I went to the Brown Pelican to talk to Miss Lavidia. If anyone knew where Miss Angel had gone to ground, she would.

I climbed the steps and knocked on the door. It was early in the afternoon and soon the deliveries would arrive for the evening. Someone should be awake. I knocked again.

The door opened, and Miss Lavidia looked out at me. "Well, well, well, if it ain't one of our local coppers. What do you need, Mr. O'Rouke?" A cigarette dangled from the corner of her mouth and she pulled her dressing gown tighter.

"I'm worried about Miss Angel. Tommy, her nephew, is real worried, too. He hasn't seen her since the fire. Any idea of where she might be?"

"You got Tommy?" She looked past me, into the street, as if she expected to see someone else.

"Yeah. He's at my place." I didn't give any more explanation.

"Hold on." She closed the door and left me on the stoop to wait. I tapped my foot, trying to keep a grip on my nerves. If I couldn't find Angel, I'd be hitting another dead end. And with Tommy's life on the line, I couldn't afford any more of those.

The door opened. "Mr. O'Rouke?" Miss Angel held the door open. "Come in, please. Tell me about Tommy." She stepped aside as I entered.

"He and his piano are with me, at my place in the Fouburg Marigny. He's safe."

"Good." She exhaled and sat on a velvet divan. "I feared for that boy."

"Miss Angel, you have to be honest with me. Do you know why anyone would want to hurt Tommy?"

"Hurt Tommy?" She stared at me.

"Look, at the raid, the coppers were looking for him. They had orders to pick him up."

"They did?" She blinked at me, and I could see the family resemblance.

"Yeah. So who would want to raid your place just to get Tommy? Think, Miss Angel." I wanted to grab her and shake her to get it out of her, and I would have, if I thought it'd help.

She shook her head.

"The bottle that came through the window was aimed at the piano. At Tommy. Someone is trying to get Tommy, and I can't keep him safe if I don't know who it is."

Angel gasped, her hands going to cover her mouth. She paled, and for a moment, I thought she'd faint. I wrapped my arm around her, and she leaned into me.

"So the fire? Tommy?" she muttered.

"Who is it? You know, don't you?" I gave her a gentle squeeze.

She sat up, patted her hair and leaned back. "If I tell you this, you can't tell Tommy. Swear to me." She took my hand in hers and looked into my eyes. "Please."

"If it's something Tommy needs to know, I can't do that. Tommy's a grown man. You can't shelter him forever."

"I know." She sighed. "I'll tell you, but if you can keep it from him, I'd appreciate it. I love that boy, and he's going to be awful upset with me."

"Why?"

"Because I lied to him." She looked like she was going to cry.

"About what?" Getting the story out was like dragging a barge up the river.

"Everything!" She burst into tears, sobbing into her hands.

God dammed women. Made me glad I didn't have to live with one. I calmed her down and held her hands. "Now, tell me from the beginning. What did you lie about?"

"His mother." She fell back against the divan. "When Tommy was old enough to ask about his mama, I told him she was my sister and had fallen on hard times. She'd come here, had him and then died."

"And that was a lie?"

"Part of it, yeah. See, she was my sister. She and I ran this place. She was…" she clamped her mouth shut and looked away.

"She was one of the working girls? A soiled dove?" Now I understood why Angel didn't want Tommy to know. The boy idolized his mother.

"Yes. She got in the family way. She always was delicate and having that baby was just too much for her. She died a few weeks after he was born. She made me swear to take care of him, raise him right, and to keep the truth about her from him."

"And you did." I gave her a hug.

"Yeah. Made up stories about her. How she loved that piano and how she played it all the time."

"Did she?" If this were a lie, it would destroy Tommy. I hoped it wouldn't be so.

"Well, she loved music. Loved to dance. She was lively, that girl. The men loved her…" She shook her head again. "She didn't leave much when she died. So I figured I'd give him something, that piano, to remember her by."

"Oh, Miss Angel." I knew my boy and this would crush him. Not just his mama being a whore, but the lie about the piano.

"I know," she wailed. "He's going to hate me!"

"Maybe, but right now, I don't think I need to tell him any of this. I don't see how it fits into who's trying to hurt him." It felt funny to know Tommy's secrets, the ones he didn't even know about. Felt like I was keeping secrets from him, and in a way, I was.

There was another secret, I could just tell, and it would be a doozey. Miss Angel was biting her lip and twisting her skirt around her finger.

"Who? Tell me."

"When his mama got in the family way, she tried to tell the father, but he wouldn't have anything to do with her. Called her a whore and told her to get rid of it."

"Tommy's father? You know who he is?"

She nodded, tears filling her eyes. "I'd hoped he'd forget about Tommy. His mama and I were the only ones who knew. Tommy doesn't know."

"But his father doesn't know that." I sat back and let my brain whirl. Someone had to be in a spot now, someone who had a lot riding on keeping Tommy out of the picture. "A name, Angel. I need a name."

"I was never sure, but his mama swore it was…Tony Fallzone."

"Fallzone? The guy running for mayor?"

She nodded. "The same. Only at the time, he was just a young man. Just starting to work for his family at the funeral home. Married, even. So when she told him she was expecting, he went nuts."

"He must know she didn't get rid of the baby."

"Yeah. He knew about the baby being born, but what could he do? And when Tommy's mama died, well, he figured that was that, I suppose. I never seen him in here again, until the night of the raid."

"Did he know you knew he was Tommy's father?" If he did, Angel's life was in danger, too.

"No. I don't think so. It was all between her and him."

Twenty years passed and now, Fallzone's rise to power meant his past couldn't come out and blindside him. He needed to get Tommy out of the picture. Either arrested or dead. Either way, he wouldn't be a problem come the election.

"You can't tell Tommy!" She grabbed my hand and held on tight.

"I won't if I don't have to. It'll destroy him. But I needed to know. Now I can protect him from Fallzone." I patted her shoulder and stood.

"Tell Tommy I'm safe, will you?"

"Of course." Something hit me. "Didn't you say you and Tommy's mother ran the Palace?"

She nodded.

"Did you both own it?"

Angel didn't meet my gaze. I took that for a yes.

"So Tommy owns part of it also."

She nodded again.

"And how long were you going to keep that a secret? How long were you going to let him stay in that little room? Pay him a pittance for playing the piano?" Now I was getting mad at her. She'd cheated Tommy out of a lot of money.

The blush rose on her face, as if she were still a virgin. "I didn't know how to tell him, not without telling him about his mother. Would the money be worth it?" She took my hand. "You care for Tommy, don't you? I can tell. I saw it when you looked at each other." She smiled.

For a moment, I thought she was threatening me and I pulled my hand away.

"No, wait! I'm just saying I'm glad! Glad for Tommy and for you. He needs someone to look out for him, and you need someone to look out for."

I still didn't answer.

"Keep him safe, Mr. O'Rouke. Now both of us know his secrets, and we both have to keep them." She smiled. Clever old broad, dragging me into her web of lies. If I told Tommy, he'd probably hate me for telling him. For Tommy, the money wouldn't be worth knowing the truth.

"I will." With that, I left.

I caught a cab back to the laundry, picked up my uniform and headed home.

To Tommy.

With my heart full of deadly secrets I swore I'd carry to my grave.

Chapter Eleven

I stood outside my house, listening to muted piano music. I could have stood there for hours taking in the amazing fact that Tommy was inside, making his music, in my house.

Then I wondered if the neighbors heard it, too. And if they did, what did they think?

I looked around, checking every house on my block and across the street. The narrow streets of the Fouburg insured that whatever noise happened, everyone heard it. Not many had their windows open. It was November, after all, and nights were chilly, even if the days warmed enough to throw open the windows.

Happy, but scared, I went up the steps and unlocked the front door.

"Hey," I said as I entered and hung up my uniform.

Tommy looked up and smiled at me. "Hey, Max, I got your note."

"Good."

"What took so long?" He never stopped playing, like his fingers just knew what to do without him telling them.

"I went to check on Miss Angel." Figured there was no reason to lie about that. I didn't like lying, especially not to Tommy. I just hoped he didn't ask me anything I'd have to lie about.

He stopped playing and turned to face me. "Is she okay?"

"Yes. She's at the Brown Pelican. Miss Lavidia took her in. I'm not sure where the other girls are, though." I sat in my chair and picked up my book, just to do something.

"I'm worried about her. What will she do without the Palace?"

"I don't know. Not sure if she knows. Not now, anyway."

"Right. I wish I could help her." He shrugged and looked down at his hands. "Max, all my stuff burned up. My clothes, my money…" His voice faded away. "I don't have a job now. I can't afford to pay rent."

"Don't worry about it, Tommy." I put down the book and smiled. "You're fine here. I have a little money put away. We can get you some new clothes."

"I don't want to do that, Max. I want to pull my weight." He looked miserable, and I hated it.

"Look. Let's call it a loan. Let me buy you some things, then, once you get a job, you can pay me back. Okay?" Every man needed his dignity, and Tommy was no exception. I'd give him whatever he needed.

He looked up, smiled, and lit up my world. Damn, the boy had me twisted up. It was nice. "Okay." He turned back to the piano and started playing this jaunty little song, letting his feelings out through his music.

"I have to go to work." I stood and got my uniform.

"Do you need me to fix you dinner?"

"Nah. James and I…"

"Right. Cops eat free." He grinned and kept on playing. "Guess I should go out later and look for another job."

I stopped dead in my tracks. "Where?" A shiver went down my spine.

"Storyville, I guess. One of the places might need a piano player."

"Why don't you wait on that a bit? There's no rush, is there? Let's enjoy some time together before you start working, okay?" It sounded good to me; I just hoped it'd sound good to him. The last thing I needed was Tommy on the streets of Storyville where someone might see him. If Fallzone was looking for him, better

Tommy stay out of sight. At least until I could figure out what to do about Fallzone.

"Sure!"

I let out the breath I was holding. "Maybe tomorrow we can go shopping for some clothes?"

"I'd like that, yeah." He pushed up his glasses.

"Good." I smiled at him, lost in those beautiful blue eyes, even behind his spectacles.

I left him to change. He played two songs as I did, and when I came out to go to work, he stopped and gave me a whistle.

"I love that uniform on you." He winked. "When I first saw you, I thought, *Who is that man? He looks good enough to eat.*"

I laughed. "No, you didn't. You thought, who's that big Irish copper?"

"That, too. But mostly, I just thought you looked handsome. Still do." He got off the kitchen chair he'd brought in to sit on while he played and came to me. "Still makes my heart go flip-flop."

It was the sweetest thing anyone had ever said to me. Tommy slayed me. How could he care for me so much? I'm nothing but a big Irish lout. Nothing special.

I pulled him into my arms. "Me, too." Then I kissed him, slow and tender, and he just melted into me. God, I loved that—the way he just surrendered to me made me feel ten feet tall. Like I could do anything.

"Gotta go." I pushed away, not wanting to leave him, but duty called.

"I'll be here." He reached up and pecked my cheek. "In bed. Naked."

Damn. My cock went stiff. "Don't say those things to me when I have to go, boy." I grabbed him by the back of the neck and pushed my tongue inside his mouth, taking a good long taste of him.

Tommy whimpered and leaned into me, his arms wrapped around my neck. I patted him on the ass, broke the kiss and took my leave.

§ § § §

I rode with James on the wagon to Storyville. He grinned at me, then turned away.

"What?" I asked, but I knew what.

He rolled his eyes. "The piano player still at your house?"

"Yeah." I stared straight ahead, hoping he'd leave it at that.

"For how long?" But no, James had to dig deeper. He was a good cop, in his own way.

"Look. I don't know. His place burned down. He's got no job." I shrugged.

"So, he's okay? You're fine with him there?" I felt his gaze on the side of my face, so I turned to him.

"I'm fine. He's fine. Drop it, okay?" We stared into each other's eyes, him trying to figure me out, and me trying not to let him see inside me.

"Fine." He huffed out a breath.

"Fine."

We rode the rest of the way in silence, until the wagon dropped us off.

"On the beat." He took out his baton and gave it a twirl, just because he knew I hate it.

"Bastard." I adjusted my cap.

"Jackass." He gave his baton a swing and then caught it under his arm.

We started our rounds in Storyville.

At the Brown Pelican, James stopped. He trotted up the steps and knocked. The Negro maid answered, and he asked for Miss Victoria. The older woman nodded and disappeared.

In her place, a beautiful mulatto came to the door. "Hi, James." She smiled up at him, all big brown eyes and café-au-lait skin. She was beautiful. His Italian family would die if they knew he loved this girl.

Just then, I got sad. For him. For me. Neither of us would be able to ever be with the ones we loved. Not in the open. Not with our families.

My family would… Well, my old man, he'd finish the job he'd started before I left, beating the crap outta me when he was drunk. My brothers would probably help him. My mother… It'd break her heart if she were still alive.

What would James' family do if they knew? Probably the same damn thing.

I watched as he talked to her, his hands straying to her waist. She played with the lapels of his uniform. To me, it looked like she cared for him, maybe even loved him. But I could see in her eyes as she said goodbye she knew it as well as I did—they could never be. She was a half-breed whore. He was an Italian copper.

It hit me. Romeo and Juliet, the star-crossed lovers. Only Storyville was their Verona. Yeah, I knew the story. Read it and a few others of Shakespeare. I never finished school, but I've always loved to read.

I wanted to ask him why he kept on with her, but I knew he would ask me the same.

Our answers would be the same—we couldn't stop. We were in love. Hopelessly.

James came down the stairs, and we continued on our way past the burned out Palace. I'd have to figure out how to get Fallzone to stop hunting Tommy. Or at least keep Tommy under wraps until after the election.

It was three weeks away. A long time to sit on my boy, keep him from going out, from anyone seeing him on the streets of Storyville, if he was going to look for another job there.

We did our beat, and as usual, things were fine. Storyville was back to normal. Gentlemen descended from carriages and automobiles, white-gloved, carrying black canes, and entered the bordellos to play with their favorite whores.

James and I stood on the corner, making our presence known. Down the block, the Brown Pelican was open and doing great business. Inside, Miss Victoria was fucking some man, maybe even giving him a suck.

How the hell could James stand that? Knowing she was with different men? If it were Tommy, I'd go crazy.

I guess I couldn't stop thinking about it. "How do you do it? Knowing she's…" It just slipped out.

He gazed down the street. "I don't think about it."

I didn't say anything. How could he not think about it? It would consume my every moment, but I just nodded.

I looked at his face and saw the truth. It killed him.

"Come on. Let's check out the next block." I pulled him away, and he dragged his feet, but came with me all the same.

We walked for a while, but I really needed to talk to someone about Tommy. Not him and me, but about what to do about Fallzone. James was my best friend. We'd been patrolling Storyville for a couple of years together, we'd gotten drunk together, and we'd been hung-over together.

It was time to trust our friendship.

"James, I gotta little problem."

"Oh, yeah?"

"It's Tommy."

"That's a big problem, Irish." He bumped into me and laughed.

Damn, what did he suspect? Probably what I didn't want him to. He was sharp enough, that was for sure.

"Look. Someone's trying to hurt him. That fire? It was meant to kill Tommy. And the raid? They were looking for him to arrest. The raid was just smoke and mirrors."

"You sure?" He frowned at me as we walked along the street.

"Yeah. So, Tommy's hiding at my place, only he doesn't know he's hiding, you get it?"

"You didn't tell him?" The shock in James' voice wormed into me.

"No. I can't. If I tell him, then I have to tell him why. And I can't do that." It was a feeble explanation, even to me.

"But you know?"

"Yeah, but I can't tell him. It'd just kill him." I tried not to sound miserable, but James wasn't having it.

"And you don't want to hurt him?" James swung his baton. Sometimes, I think in order for his brain to work, he had to swing it.

"No."

Silence. We walked another half-block before he spoke. "Max, you're my best friend…you know that." I nodded. "So you know I have to tell you you're playing with fire." He lowered his voice. "You could go to jail, Max."

"I know."

He sighed. "We're a pair, huh?"

"Yeah." I chuckled. He chuckled, then before I could stop it, we were laughing as if it was the funniest thing we'd ever heard. But it was the saddest. Guess laughing was better than crying.

He clapped me on the back as he sobered. "Your secret's safe with me, Max."

"You're being sort of noble about it. Figured you'd report me or ask for a new partner." I couldn't look at him right then, afraid to see what might be in his eyes.

"Naw. I'd have to break someone new in." He shrugged. "Besides, you don't say anything about Victoria, and I know a lot of guys would, her being a whore and half-Negro. Guess I have my secrets, too."

"Guess so."

We walked.

"Thanks, James."

"You, too."

"Now, what do I do about Tommy?"

"Chain him to that damn piano?" James laughed. "How long do you have to keep him hidden?" I liked that James didn't ask any more, that he didn't dig any deeper.

"Three weeks."

He whistled. "That's a long time. Maybe he could leave the city?"

"Where? And he doesn't have any money. What little he had, burned in the Palace."

"Damn." James squinted, giving me his thinking face. "You got any relatives you could send him to?"

"Without telling him why? No. My family is all here or back in Ireland. And the ones here…well, I don't want them to know about Tommy. What about you? Can I hide him with your people?"

James stopped and ran his hand over his chin. "Most of my people are back in Italy, same as you. I got a sister, she lives in the Vieux Carre. Her husband runs a little grocery store on Decatur Street. Maybe if I talk to her, he could work there for a few weeks."

"Really? That'd work." Or would it? Hiding Tommy with the Italians? He'd have to use another name. It was the best I could do right now. "Can you ask?"

"Sure. Can't hurt to ask. She's always complaining they need help."

"Thanks."

"Don't thank me yet. Marie's gotta say yes first. I'll drop by the shop tomorrow and ask, then I'll let you know."

We did the rest of the rounds for the night and when our replacements showed up, we took their place on the wagon and rode back to the station. After we clocked in, James headed home and so did I.

Chapter Twelve

No piano music met me when I walked up to my house. Something tasting very much like fear coated the back of my throat. I swallowed hard, trying to dislodge it, but it stayed. There were no lights from behind the wooden shutters on the front window. The place looked empty.

"I told him to not to go out," I muttered, as I trotted up the steps to the front door. I wanted to shake him, yell at him, but I was too afraid I'd find him gone, instead of just asleep.

I let myself in. The front room was dark.

"Tommy?" I called out. Half-mad, half-scared, my voice didn't sound like my own.

I paused to listen. Silence. I was going to kill him. He'd disobeyed me, and it made something deep inside me turn on, like an electric light.

I strode down the hall, past the dark kitchen, the closed bathroom door, to my bedroom. The door was shut.

It flew open when I hit it and crashed into the wall with a bang.

"What?" a voice screeched from the darkened room.

"Tommy?" I stood panting in the doorway, furious and terrified at the same time.

"Max? What's going on?" Tommy sat up in my bed, rubbing his eyes.

I slumped against the doorframe, my knees nearly giving out.

"Thank God."

He sat up, swung his legs over the side of the bed, and stared at me. "For what? Scaring the hell outta me?" Now he looked pissed.

I laughed and ran my hand over my face. "For being here."

"Where else would I be?" He fell back on the bed. "Jesus, Max, I was having a great dream."

"About me?" Now that I got a good look and the fear had left, I enjoyed what I saw—Tommy stretched out, naked, his cock half-hard, his hair tousled from sleep, and no glasses. Nothing looked finer, unless when he'd just been fucked. By me.

"Yeah. We were—" He broke off and stroked his cock. "It felt very…er…real."

"Dreams are nice. Ready for the real thing?" I took off my jacket, my shirt, and kicked off my shoes. I held his gaze as I dropped the suspenders of my trousers and got out of them and my drawers. Only my socks stayed on. The house was chilly, but despite it, my erection didn't retreat.

Tommy gave me this little smile, the one that says he wanted to be naughty. The one that twisted me up inside. That made me hard as steel.

"Against the headboard." I advanced, closing in on him and the bed. *Him in my bed.* God, just the thought of it got me harder.

He scooted backward until his back hit the headboard. "Like this?"

"Yeah. Gonna make your dreams come true, boy."

Tommy's prick stood at attention, straight and strong. The nearly purple head got my lust rising, and I had to touch myself as I crawled onto the bed. I straddled his legs and grabbed the top of the headboard.

Rising up, I positioned my cock in front of his face. "Suck me, boy." I looked down at him as he leaned his head back to meet my gaze. Hunger. Lust. Love.

He took me at the base with his hand and opened his mouth.

Guiding me forward, he rubbed my cock all over his lips, around in a circle, and used his tongue to swipe it every now and then.

"Tommy," I whispered, then clamped my mouth shut, afraid too much would come out about the way he made me feel. About how I felt for him.

He closed his lips around me, moaned, and then started to suck me. God, the boy could do this just fine. Finer than any dollar whore I'd ever used. I looked down at where my cock slid in and out of his mouth and shuddered. What a fucking sight.

I moved faster, thrusting into his wetness, holding onto the bed for balance and leverage. I wanted to unleash on him, really let go and slam deep into his mouth, but I didn't want to hurt him or scare him. He wasn't a whore. He was my lover, and I wanted to treat him as such, with love, warmth, and tenderness. But I also wanted to fuck him into the mattress.

He held my hips with his hands, his thumbs digging into my belly. I groaned, just thinking of him touching me, and he must have read my mind, because just then, he let go with one hand and grabbed my ass. He kneaded it, squeezing and palming it, and each time, he moved his fingers closer to the valley between my cheeks.

I'd never let anyone touch me there. I fucked and got sucked. But something about Tommy, something about how I felt about him, and I don't know. I wanted him to touch me there. Wanted to feel him press against my hole, maybe even get inside me.

That scared the hell outta me. I pulled back, but he soothed me with his hands and mouth, and I relaxed into it. Letting him stroke me again, swiping down the cleft, up and down, until I'd gotten used to it, and all the while sucking me just hard enough, but easy enough not to make me come.

I pushed back onto his fingers, telling him it was okay for him to touch me there. Who was I kidding? It was more than okay. I wanted it bad. He pushed his fingertip deeper and found my hole. He played with it, rubbing it, feeling all around it, driving me outta my head with needing him inside me.

"Tommy. God. Feels so good." And it did. I understood why

Tommy and the others liked it. It felt amazing, like all my nerves concentrated on that one spot and along my cock and inside my balls…like they were all one and the same.

He stopped touching me, and I looked down to see what was going on. He opened his mouth and added his finger along side my cock, wetting it. Slicking it up. A thrill shot through me, knowing what he was preparing to do.

Put his finger inside me.

I groaned. "Tommy, yes. Do it." I thrust harder, unable to control myself. Tommy did something to me, made it easy to drop my guard, let down my defenses, and let him in. In my heart and in my body.

He breached me, sliding his finger in, then with a quick twist, he pulled it out.

I gasped, from shock and pleasure, a fine mix of the two, but I wanted more. I pushed back again, and he slipped inside me again, this time deeper.

He still sucked me, but he'd let go and his other hand pulled at the other cheek of my ass, moving it out of the way so he could run his fingers up and down the valley.

I was surrounded, my walls breached, the head of my cock deep in his territory and his finger deep in mine.

There was nothing left but to give in, to lay down arms and surrender.

He pushed deeper still and found that spot inside a man. Found my trigger switch and rubbed it, and just like that, I gave in and gave up.

I came, crying and arching and shooting down his throat as my channel squeezed his finger, sucking it in deeper, and all the nerves in my body focused on my genitals.

A hot splash hit my balls and thighs, and that sent another shiver of ecstasy through me. He'd come on me, just from sucking me and touching me. His body vibrated as he moaned through it.

"Oh, Max, I love you."

"Tommy. God. Yes," I whispered as he buried his face against my belly and held me tight. I sat down on his legs, catching my breath, trying to understand what he'd said. What I'd said or didn't say.

I leaned forward and touched our foreheads together. "Never let anyone touch me like that before."

"I never touched anyone like that before either." He smiled, and I had to kiss him. Slow and soft and loving. It was new to me, this loving feeling, this tenderness for someone—another man—but I didn't fight it. It was what it was and that was enough for me.

I climbed off him and drew us both down so we lay face to face in the dark room, only the light from the open door to illuminate us.

"You scared me. When I got home and the place was dark, I'd thought you'd left." I stroked the side of his face.

"I thought I'd save us money on the fuel bill. Since I don't have a job right now." He shrugged and kissed me back.

"Don't worry about it. I have enough. And I talked to someone today about finding you a job in the Vieux Carre. It's not much, but it's something for now."

"Really?" He grinned and pushed up on one elbow. "Playing piano?"

"No." And his smile fell.

"Oh." He paused, then shook his head. "Sorry. What is it? I'll take anything."

I wanted to tell him it was only for a few weeks, just until after the election, but I couldn't without saying why that was important. I'd sworn to keep his secret, even from him.

"Right. Just for now. To tide us over, that's all. Until you find your music job." I hurried to explain myself. "I knew you felt like you wanted to not stay here free and all. Thought if you had a job, any job, you'd feel better about staying here. Not want to leave or anything."

"Max, I never want to leave. You've got to know that by now. Don't you?" He touched my cheek. "You're stuck with me." He cleared his throat. "Unless you don't want me." His gaze told me he worried about that.

"I want you. Now and for as long as you'll have me." I looked down and took a breath. "No one has ever told me they loved me, unless it was my ma."

"Really? How can that be? Haven't you had any other lovers? I can't be your first. You're too…experienced." He looked at me, that shy smile on his face.

"Not a lover. Not like you. Lots of fucks and sucks. But they were all whores. No names. I paid them and, most of the time, never saw them again." I gave a half-laugh. "So, yeah, you are my first. My first true love." There, I'd said it. Confessed it to him.

The smile on his face just got bigger and bigger and as it grew, so did my heart, until if felt like it would burst right outta my chest.

"True love. I like that." He threw his arms around my neck, pulled me down on top of him, and kissed me like there was no tomorrow.

I didn't say it, but I felt it. *Me, too.*

Chapter Thirteen

The next week, Tommy started the job at the Italian grocery store over on Decatur and he couldn't have been happier…well, doing something that wasn't playing his piano. He did that plenty when he got home and today was no exception. I'd trotted down the steps to the beat of some upbeat jazz tune as I headed off to work.

Old Lady Riley, the widow from across the street, called to me from behind the iron fence around her tiny bricked front yard. Her husband had been a fireman and died in a fire ten years ago.

"Officer O'Rouke!" A white hankie fluttered at me as she waved it.

I crossed the street to her. "Yes, ma'am?"

"That young man? The one playing the piano all day long?" She squinted at me through the spectacles perched on her nose.

"Is the music bothering you?" I asked, to be nice. I'd hate to tell Tommy not to play so loudly, but if the neighbors complained, he'd have to tone it down. I didn't want anyone asking me questions about him, like the coppers.

"No! I enjoy it. Sometimes I sit on my stoop and listen." She winked at me. "I been meaning to ask…is he moving in? Or just visiting?"

"He's down on his luck, and I let him bunk with me." That was vague enough.

"Oh, that's nice of you." She smiled at me and patted my arm.

"You're truly a good man."

I shrugged. "He's paying part of the rent, so in a way he's helping me, too." The truth of Tommy and my relationship I couldn't even think about in her presence without turning beet red. If I said anything, she'd probably keel over dead.

"Good. Rent is expensive these days. I barely get by with my late husband's pension."

Her pension? A paltry sum every month from the Beneficent Society of Firemen. She was too old to do more than take in a little sewing on the side. It broke my heart. And I knew for sure some of the ladies in the neighborhood gave her food and such every now and then.

"It's hard for everyone. And with the war?" I shook my head.

"It's lucky you didn't have to fight." She patted me again.

"Well, I wanted to." And I had. "But the city needs cops. Can't have us all running off to fight a war overseas, can we?" I grinned at her. "Who would look after you?"

"Indeed, we do. Why, I feel so much safer knowing you live right across the street." This time, she batted her lashes at me like a young lady.

"I have to go…duty calls." I tipped my hat to her and walked off. At the corner, I turned and glanced back. She was leaning on the fence, listening to Tommy's music.

If he gave her some happiness, I guess that was okay. Maybe the other neighbors wouldn't complain either. Maybe Tommy's music brought a little happiness into everyone's life.

He sure brought it to mine.

§ § § §

The Pleasure Palace wouldn't re-open. Word on the street was Miss Angel didn't have the cash to rebuild. I wondered if she would relocate somewhere in Storyville, but no one spoke of it.

And I hadn't seen her at the Brown Pelican either.

Something inside me said maybe she'd moved on. Picked up and headed somewhere new. Like Atlanta, Jackson, or maybe Mobile. I wondered if she'd had the sense to grab the cash before the place burned down. I also wondered how much of that money should have belonged to Tommy.

If I saw her again, I was going to ask her.

As the election for mayor neared, Storyville changed. The atmosphere of the place dimmed a bit. Everyone talked and speculated about what a new mayor would mean to the area or, if the old mayor won, would he keep things the same or would he buckle under to his wife's insistence that he shut down the "den of inequity and sin" forever?

The gentry still came, but not as much as before. The raid and the fire had tarnished the good-time feeling of the district. Or maybe they saw the tide changing.

I only had a week to go before the election and Tommy would be safe. I hoped and prayed. I also knew if Fallzone won the election, he'd still be looking for Tommy. Maybe even harder. The re-election of the old mayor for a second term was my only hope.

At that point, I didn't care if his saintly wife shut the whole city down, as long as my boy was safe and could play his piano until the cows came home.

But Tommy…he grew restless. The grocery store wasn't what he was used to— beautiful women, dressed in the finest undergarments, classy furniture, gentlemen asking him to play a song for them, putting tips in his glass jar. Instead, he was stocking shelves and hauling goods out to the wagons and automobiles.

Because he only worked part of the day, the little he made at the grocery must have looked to be a pittance, but it was honest work. Not that his playing wasn't honest, despite being in a whorehouse. I wasn't going to say that to Tommy. He'd take my face off if I did.

The boy had a temper.

Three days before the election, I got up late and Tommy wasn't home. He didn't sleep late, like me. For a man who played piano until the wee hours of the morning, he didn't have a problem getting up early. Most days he'd be up, dressed and fed before I got up.

And he'd be ready to go to work at the grocery store, too. He left around ten in the morning and walked to work. I figured it was safe since it was nowhere near Storyville. Fallzone couldn't search the entire city, could he?

However, today I got a weird feeling in the pit of my belly. Fear, I suppose. Worry, too.

It only grew as I walked through the house calling for him and getting no answer.

I stood in the front room, confused. Then I walked through it again, looking for a note, but Tommy hadn't left one. Time was passing and I got dressed for work, but didn't know what to do after that. He usually returned from work around three in the afternoon; they only needed him for the mid-day rush. We'd spend a few minutes together before I left, like ships in the night, stealing a few kisses and caresses before we parted.

But here it was a quarter past three and still no Tommy. I ground my teeth together as the worry built inside me. I paced the front room, slapping my baton against my palm. By now, he'd usually be sitting at the piano, playing. Teasing me as I got dressed. Promising me he'd do wicked things to me and let me do nasty things to him when I got home.

It scared me at how fast I'd come to expect him to be here. How fast he'd become part of my life and how much I needed him.

I put my baton away, threw myself into my chair and picked up my book, but just couldn't focus enough to read. The idea that Fallzone had picked my boy up kept popping up in my head. Tommy being dragged off down some dark alley by Fallzone's men played over and over, until I was sure that's what had happened to him.

I'd have to leave to go on duty soon, and the idea of not knowing where my boy was all shift drove me even crazier. I went over and over my decision not to tell him about Fallzone. Maybe I'd made a big mistake. Maybe I should've told him to stay away from Storyville. Made up some excuse. Anything to get him to stay put and safe.

At three-thirty, the key sounded in the lock and Tommy breezed in.

I jumped outta my chair and yelled, "Where the hell have you been?"

Tommy stared at me, mouth open. "Work."

"Uh-uh." I shook my head. "Before work. You were gone when I got up. And no note."

He glanced at my hands balled into hard fists and he stepped back. "I didn't think I'd be gone so long." He licked his lips and his gaze darted all over, anywhere but me. Part of it was fear, but another part was pure guilt.

I knew something was up.

"Where have you been?" This time I calmed my voice down.

He swallowed. "Storyville. I went to see Miss Angel."

"Holy hell!" I threw the book down. Tommy jerked back.

"What the hell is wrong with you?" he shouted, and from the look of dismay on his face, I was going to have to explain my temper tantrum. Then that look changed. His brows furrowed and his eyes narrowed.

"Wait! Why should I feel bad? What's wrong with that?" He put his hands on his hips and cocked his head to the side. "You telling me I can't go somewhere without your permission?"

Oh hell, I'd riled my boy up. "No, of course not."

"Damn right. I'm not your property. I can come and go as I please, and today it pleased me to go to talk to Miss Angel." He crossed his arms over his chest and glared at me.

"Did you find her?" Part of me dreaded his answer.

"No." He sagged, went to his piano and sat down. He played a few notes, sort of half-hearted and sad. I wanted to wrap him up in my arms and keep him safe. "She's gone."

"What do you mean, gone?" Guess my tone was too gruff because he flinched, so I softened my voice. "From Storyville?"

"From New Orleans." He looked about ready to burst into tears. "She was my only relative. My aunt. How could she just leave without telling me? Not even a goodbye note."

"Aw, boy, I'm sorry." *The bitch.* Skipped town and probably with Tommy's share of the money. I went over to him and pulled him up and into my arms.

He sagged against me. "She was like a mother to me, Max. My connection to my real mother. Now, I don't even have her." The tears flowed.

Tommy sobbed into my chest, dampening my work shirt, but I let him, until he was done. He sniffed and pulled away. "Sorry. You're going to be late for work." He brushed my shirt off and stepped back.

"I'll catch a cab, so don't worry." I wiped the tears off his face with my thumbs and kissed his sweet lips.

It seemed to be over, when he asked, "But Max? Why were you so mad at me?"

I closed my eyes and tried half a truth. "It's dangerous. Tommy, I think someone was trying to get you outta the way."

"Out of the way of what? What are you talking about?" He pulled out of my arms.

"Remember the night of the raid? The cop that said to make sure to capture you?"

Tommy nodded.

"Well, why? I wondered about that for days. Why did they want you? So I did some snooping. You were the only one they really wanted, and to get you, they had to raid the place. You're not exactly a criminal, Tommy."

He stared at me. "That's crazy. What have I done? I just play the piano." He shrugged. "And who wanted me arrested?"

Now that was the problem, wasn't it? If I told him, the rest of the truth would have to come out. I wanted to keep that secret as long as I had to, if I could help it.

"Not sure."

He narrowed his eyes again. "Yes, you are. Max, I know you. You're smart. I know you figured it out. Who wants me arrested?"

I swallowed. "I'm not that smart. Haven't figured it out." I turned away from his intense gaze.

"You're lying." The accusation in his voice slammed into me. And that he knew me so well he could tell I lied frightened me. No one had ever been that close to me. Even as a kid, neither my mother nor my old man could tell when I lied.

"I don't know what you're talking about." I was desperate to keep it from him, so I dug myself into a trench.

He stared at me, then he shook his head. Without a word, he headed to the back room.

"Where are you going?" I called. I needed to finish this argument and get to work.

"I'm leaving," he shouted back at me just before the bedroom door slammed shut.

Chapter Fourteen

Leaving?

Like I'd been hit with my own baton, I staggered to my chair and fell into it.

Tommy couldn't be serious. He couldn't be leaving me.

I stared down the hall as questions raced through my mind.

Where would he go? What would he do? Was there someone else he could go to? Someone else who wanted him, like I wanted him?

And what the hell was I going to do with a piano?

Tommy had to be joking. He was in a pique, that's all. Once he calmed down, he'd see reason. He'd stay.

The bedroom door opened and he stomped down the hall, my beat-up old suitcase in his hand. *Holy hell!*

I bolted out of the chair and stopped him at the doorway to the front room, both of my hands on his shoulders.

"What are you doing?" I searched his face, but saw only determination and fury.

"I'm leaving."

"But where are you going?" I shook him. "You don't have anywhere to go."

"I'll find someplace. I'm sure someone in Storyville will give me a room in exchange for work." He shook me off, and I let my hands fall to my sides.

When he tried to move forward, I blocked his path. He wasn't leaving, and he sure as hell wasn't going to Storyville.

I put my hand on his chest and pushed him back. "Hell, no. You're staying right here."

He knocked my hand away. "I might be your boy, Max, but I'm not your slave." I'd never heard such anger in his voice. Such resolve.

"You *are* my boy, Tommy. And I want to protect you." I tried to reason with him.

"From what?" he screeched. "From who? Why won't you tell me? It's my life, Max. I should know what the hell is going on! I can't stand being treated like a child. I'm a grown man." He vibrated, his chin wavering, his eyes liquid.

"I don't know," I shouted.

"Fuck that! You're lying! I won't stay with someone who lies to me. Get out of my way, Max." He glared at me, chin raised, daring me to stop him.

I was lying. And he knew it.

I didn't know what to do, what to say, how to stop him.

"You can't leave!"

He stepped around me, and something inside me snapped. I grabbed his arm as he passed and twisted it, up and behind his back. He yelped and dropped the suitcase, then twisted around and punched me in the jaw. "Fuck you!"

My vision blurred and pain burst through my face. The boy had a mean right hook.

But I never lost my grip on him. I shook my head to clear it and grabbed his free arm, twisting it with the other one. Now, he was pinned, with my hand holding him helpless.

He tried to kick me, and I laughed. At least I knew he could hold his own in a fight.

"Stop it. Let me go, you bastard!" He struggled, but I had pounds and inches on him, and my ire was up. My blood was up, too, and it filled my cock.

I pushed him face first into the wall, then pressed my body into his, nestling my cock against his ass. "Listen to me. Calm down," I whispered in his ear.

He stopped moving, but said nothing.

Guess it was my turn to speak, if I could get any blood back to my brain. Right then, I wanted nothing more than to shove down his trousers and fuck him against the wall. If we were playing, I'd do it and know he wanted it, but now? He was pissed at me and probably wasn't thinking the way I was, and I'd never force him. Never.

I had to tell him, but it made my belly ache something awful. I thought I might throw up, just knowing what he might do.

"You want the truth?"

"Yes!"

"I didn't want to tell you. For the last time, it's better kept a secret. Can't you trust me about this?" I pleaded.

He didn't answer for a moment and then he whispered, "No, Max. I need to know. I need you to treat me like an equal. Like a grown man, not a boy. If I'm in danger, if my life is threatened, I need to know."

I buried my face in the back of his neck and inhaled him. "I love you, Tommy."

"I know, Max."

"I don't want you to hate me."

"Why would I hate you?"

"You will. When I tell you the truth. And then you'll leave, and I—"

"I won't leave."

"You will." I didn't recognize my own voice for the rasp in it.

"No, I swear it."

"I need you, boy." That was God's truth. But I was afraid I needed him more than he needed me. That it'd be easy for him to walk away from me.

"I need you, Max. Now, let me go and tell me the truth."

I sighed. He might think he'd forgive me for telling him his mother was a whore, but I knew better. He'd built his mother up to be a saint.

I stepped back and let him go. He let his arms fall and then turned around, still leaning against the wall for support. This time, when he looked at me, there wasn't any anger, only concern.

"What could be so bad, Max?"

I took his hand and led him into the bedroom. "Sit down."

Tommy sat on the edge of the bed. "Okay. I'm sitting. Now tell me." He licked his lips and fear flickered in his gaze. I thought he was the bravest man I knew. And I was the biggest coward.

Well, if he could listen to the truth, I could tell it.

"There's a man, Anthony Fallzone, and he's running for mayor. Have you heard of him?"

Tommy shook his head. "I don't follow that stuff much."

"Well, he's got a few bodies in his closet. And you're one of them."

Tommy frowned. "You're not making sense, Max."

I paced a bit, then turned to him. "Look. This all begins with the Pleasure Palace."

"The Palace?"

"Yeah. Before you were born, Miss Angel ran a little whorehouse. Before Storyville grew into what it is now. And she had a partner." I stopped and wiped my face with both hands. Damn, this was hard.

I knelt down in front of him and took his hands. "Tommy, your mother was her partner."

The scowl on Tommy's face would have withered a rose. His brows knitted together, and he stared down at our linked hands. "No. My mother wasn't around then."

"Yes, she was. I talked to Angel. She and your mother were partners. And were, until the day your mother died. That's why you were born at the Palace. It's where she lived. It's where she worked." I sat back on my heels and watched him take it in.

"No," he whispered. "She was visiting my aunt when she had me."

"Not according to Angel. Your mother got pregnant by one of the…clients."

Tommy snapped his head up and glared at me. "Clients? No! That's not true."

"Why would Angel lie to me?"

"Why would she lie to me?" he shouted.

"Because she didn't want you growing up, knowing that your mother was a…whore."

The breath whooshed out of Tommy's chest, fanning my face, and he stared into my eyes.

"No. Liar. You're just saying this…because…" Tears filled his blue eyes, and my heart just broke.

"Because it's true. Your mother worked, just like Angel did, in the early days."

"My mother?" Tommy covered his face with his hands as he shook.

"Now, listen to me, boy. Doesn't matter what she did or didn't do. That's not the point. The point is the man who thinks he's your father is Fallzone."

Tommy stilled. "My father? Fallzone? Italian?"

"Right. So he's running for mayor. He's married, got a family, runs a nice funeral business. What he doesn't need is an illegitimate son showing up, fucking it all up for him."

"Me?" Tommy sniffled and wiped his nose with his sleeve.

"You. So he figures if he can get you outta the picture, get you arrested, maybe even arrange for an accident, then all the evidence would be gone."

"But the only person who knew about this was Angel. Why

would he go after me?"

"Because maybe he thinks you know he's your daddy."

He raised his head and blinked. "Is that why Angel disappeared?"

"Yeah. I talked to her, and she said she didn't think Fallzone believed she knew the truth, but I'm not sure about that. I guess she figured she better get outta town or she'd end up like you. I believe Fallzone burned down the Palace to try to kill you and I think she decided she'd be safer long gone."

"What about me?" Tommy's gaze hardened.

"She left you to fend for yourself. She also left with all the money from the Palace. Money that was, by rights, partly yours." He had to know all of it, even if it destroyed his feelings for me.

"My aunt cheated me? All these years?" he wailed, but I heard the anger in it.

He pushed me aside and jumped up. Striding over to the wall, he slammed his fist against it. "Fuck!"

"Tommy, I'm so sorry."

He spun around and his gaze shot daggers at me.

"My aunt swindled me. My mother was a whore. What else, Max? Gonna tell me you don't love me?"

"No! I love you. I tried to keep this from you. I tried to keep you safe, but you had to go out, go looking for Angel, go into Storyville!" I reached for him, but he danced away.

"No! You knew. How long have you known? Were you *ever* going to tell me? Were you just going to let me go on believing the lies?" Tears spilled over and tracked down his cheeks.

"Honestly? Yeah. I'd have kept those secrets 'til I died, if it meant you not being hurt. I'd do anything to keep you safe, boy. You gotta know that."

Tommy looked at the floor for a long time. He exhaled and then came to me. He took my hand and brought it to his lips. "I know."

"But you gave me no choice. There's only a few more days until the election. If the mayor wins, you're safe, but if Fallzone wins…"

He shot his gaze up to mine and his lips parted. "If he wins, what then?"

"Then I guess we need to leave New Orleans." I shrugged.

"Leave?"

"Well, you'll never be safe. You'd still be a danger to him and need to be removed. New Orleans wouldn't be safe for you."

"But you said 'we'?"

"Yeah. You're not going anywhere without me."

"But your job here?"

"There's coppers in every city, boy. I can get a job."

"And I can play the piano anywhere, too."

"Sure." I gathered him into my arms, and he held on tight.

"Max!" He pushed me away. "You'll be late for work!"

"Fuck!" I pulled out my pocket watch. "Gotta go!" I dashed to the front room, grabbed my jacket and pulled it on. "Don't leave, understand?"

Tommy nodded.

"You'll be here when I get back?" I needed him to say yes.

He smiled. "Waiting you for, Max. Right here."

"And you don't hate me? For telling you?" I prayed he'd say no, so I held my breath and waited.

"Max, I love you. I guess, maybe, deep down inside, I knew it. Knew what she was."

"I'm so sorry."

"Me, too."

"See you tonight?" I opened the door.

"Tonight." He nodded, and I tore myself away.

The entire time I rushed to work, I kept thanking God my boy still loved me.

I clocked in late, then met up with James on his way out of the station. As we patrolled Storyville, I kept thinking of how I was going to show Tommy just how much I loved him once I got home.

Chapter Fifteen

Election day finally arrived, and both Tommy and I woke up early. Don't need to say it, but we voted for the incumbent mayor. It was the least we could do to help Fallzone lose and keep Tommy safe. Even James promised he'd vote against the man, despite them both being Italian.

I don't know what Tommy was thinking, but I worried about where we'd go if Fallzone won. I'd promised Tommy we'd pack up and leave.

Looking around my house, there wasn't much to leave.

Tommy played his piano off and on, and when he passed it he'd touch it, running his fingers over the keys, picking at where the varnish had peeled off, like he was trying to remember everything about it.

We'd know who won in the morning, when the *Picayune* came out. The winner would be splashed all over the front page.

We'd either dance or pack.

That morning, we moved from the kitchen for food, to the bed for pleasure. I'd already fucked him when we woke, and he'd sucked my cock before lunch.

After lunch, we found ourselves back in bed. Tommy had cooked us bacon and scrambled eggs. He did breakfast best, so we ate it a lot. Not that I'm complaining. He makes good eggs. But our bellies were full and we drowsed, not quite asleep and not quite awake.

It was peaceful under the covers with him. His warm, naked body pressed against mine. His delicate hand, with its long fingers curled on my chest, had a weight that soothed me, and his soft breathing against the side of my neck aroused me.

I was happy. Happier than I could remember ever being since I was a kid and a new ball at Christmas could make me feel joyous. Tommy gave that to me.

What did I give to Tommy? Did he feel the same happiness? It was hard to tell because he'd been so upset about his mother and his aunt he'd moped for days, though he tried to hide it. I'd catch him staring off into the air, like he was thinking or seeing something I couldn't. When he caught me watching, he'd laugh and kiss me, or play the piano for me as I read my book.

But right now, in this moment, I believed I made him happy. Even asleep, he smiled, and I hoped he was dreaming of me, like I dreamed of him.

Most of my dreams weren't dirty; they were just us laughing and having a good time. Here in the house, or on a cab ride, or walking down the streets.

He opened his eyes and looked up into mine. "Hi." He smiled that wicked smile that twisted me up inside. "Need you."

"Need you." And I did. Like I needed the air to breath and the sun to shine.

I rolled on top of him and kissed him, deep, with my tongue, as I searched out all the places and tastes he held in secret just for me. He moaned and arched up into me, and we rubbed our cocks together.

Wonderful friction! Soft as velvet and hard as iron. Both of us grunting and rutting against each other like stags on does. And when we finally came, the splash of my cum against his belly and his all over mine, only made me happier.

I guess the grin on my face gave me away.

"Happy?" he asked, as he snuggled into my arms again.

"Yes. You?"

"Like crazy." He kissed my jaw and gave it a nip. "Never dreamed I could be this happy."

"Me, too." I fell silent as I looked at the clock on my nightstand. I didn't have work this evening. We could spend all our time here in bed, if we wanted.

"Max."

"Yeah."

"Do you think Angel will ever come back?" He drew circles in the hair on my chest.

"No, I don't."

"Oh." The resignation in his voice saddened me.

"Do you miss her?" I suppose he did, being she was his only family for his whole life.

"Funny. Not really." He smirked. "Guess I'm still mad at her for not telling me the truth and for using me all those years as cheap labor."

"She never paid you, did she? All you made was the tips, right?" I'd suspected as much. Something about Angel told me she was a cheap old broad.

"No. She let me stay in the room and keep my tips. I make better money at the grocery." He laughed and kissed me. "If we move, I can work in a grocery store and play the piano in a bar."

"And I can walk a beat anywhere."

"But you wanted to be a detective. Will you have to start over?" He frowned as he rested his chin on my chest and looked at me.

"Probably not. I have to take the detective's test, get a recommendation, that sort of thing. It might take a year or two extra, but I can still do it."

"Max."

"Yeah?"

"How will we move the piano?" His expectant look shot right to my heart. Why did I always have to hurt him? Tell him what he didn't want to hear?

"We can't. At least, not if we want to get outta here fast and in secret."

"Oh. Right." He sighed. "Guess dragging a piano with us would be dead giveaway."

"Yeah." I hugged him and tousled his hair. "But there might be a way, if we shipped it on the train."

"That's a good idea!" Tommy smiled, and his face lit up like the sun hit it full on.

"Let's slow down, okay? We don't know what's going to happen until tomorrow morning."

"Right." He looked around the room. "I like this room, Max. I like this house. I want to stay here, if we can."

"Me, too, but if we can't, we can't. It's that simple. I'm not going to take a chance on Fallzone finding you and hurting you, just to save his stupid political career."

"My hero!" He threw his arms around me and kissed me hard.

I chuckled at his possessiveness and rolled him over on top of me.

He sat up, straddled across my waist, then backed up until my cock rubbed against the valley of his ass. He wiggled, the tease, and my cock hardened fast.

"Oh, Max, I want you to fuck me."

"Want you to ride me."

I reached for the bottle of oil on the bedside table and poured some into my hand. Then I slicked my cock up, to ease my way in. My fingers were coated with oil and it made it easy for me to slip one inside Tommy's hole.

It tightened, then let me in, and he moaned so sweetly. "Yes, Max. Deeper."

I couldn't resist going deeper, hitting the spot that excited him. I massaged the bump, and he just about vibrated right off me.

His cock stood straight up against his belly, and I had to see more. "Touch your prick, boy. Show me how you like it."

Tommy obeyed. I loved when he did that, without questions or arguments. He worked his hand up and down the slender shaft, pushing a drop of pre-cum out. It stretched from his tip to my belly before it broke and landed on me.

I had to fuck him now.

"Ride me. Now. Get on my cock." I held him as he rose up on his knees so I could position my cock under him. Then, eyes closed, blissful smile in place, he lowered his body down.

I pushed up, my cock pressuring his entrance, demanding he let me in. I groaned when I slipped inside. As he worked his way down on me, we both moaned with the pleasure.

"Love watching you, boy." I did. He excited me in ways I'd never imagined.

"Love you fucking me, Max." He groaned as he settled on my groin, every inch of me inside him. His legs were spread wide to give me more room, and he'd leaned forward with his hands resting on my chest.

"Kiss me." I reached up and pulled him down to me by the back of his neck.

His kiss was sweet, but demanding, like if he didn't get his tongue inside my mouth, he'd die. I let him in, and he took possession of it, tasting and licking everywhere, until he captured my tongue and sucked it hard.

He played with fire, trying to get rough with me. I slapped his ass with one hand, and he cried out, "Yes! Again!"

So I spanked him as I fucked him, each slap landing at the top of my thrust. He rode me, took my slaps, jerked his cock and kept whimpering like a needy puppy.

"Max! Want to come!"

"Not yet." I wanted to control him, and he wanted to be controlled.

He hissed and nodded, still riding me, still working his cock, as he gazed into my eyes, begging me silently to give him permission.

I waited until I was right on the edge, my balls tight to my body, ready to unload into him, then I said, "Do it. Come for me."

"Max!" His body tensed and his channel tightened around my cock, squeezing it hard, just like I liked it. God, he was warm and tight and so beautiful, I thought my heart would break. He did it to me, broke my heart every time I made love to him.

I just couldn't believe a beautiful man like him could love a big lout like me.

I couldn't let anything happen to him. He'd already had a hard life, not that I'd had such a good life, but I knew I could do for him what no one else could—protect and love him.

He came, shooting lines of cum all over my belly as he shuddered and moaned.

It was dirty and exciting and sent me right over.

I exploded, emptying into him, giving him my all, my everything, my essence as I tried to get so deep inside him I could feel his heart beating.

Tommy slid down, resting on my chest, his cum between us, sealing our bodies together. I softened and slipped out of him, the sudden coldness hitting my sensitive cock. I dragged the cover over us, and Tommy shifted to the side, his arms still around my neck.

"Love you, boy."

"Love you, Max."

I kissed him. "Get some sleep."

"Won't be able to sleep. Too nervous." He snuggled his face into my neck.

I grinned, knowing he'd be out in a few minutes. He was like a puppy, all get up and go and then he'd collapse into a deep sleep.

Faster than I figured, his soft breathing told me he'd fallen asleep.

But he was right. I was too nervous to sleep.

I kept running over and over what I had to do if Fallzone won. Pack. Resign. Buy train tickets. Get the damned piano shipped.

And most importantly, figure out where we were going to go to set up our new lives.

§ § § §

I must have fallen asleep sometime during the night because I woke up with sunlight coming through the curtains.

"Tommy, get up!" I shook him by the shoulder. He'd buried himself next to me under the covers.

"Hmm?" He blinked and rubbed his eyes, just like a little kid.

Damn, why did he have to do that sort of thing, making me love him more and more?

"It's morning. Time to find out who won." I sat up and started to dress. "We can go down the street to Esplanade Avenue. They have a newsstand there."

"Right." He groaned and climbed out of bed. "Be back." He padded to the bathroom.

I had on my trousers and shirt by the time he returned, so I took a piss and met him in the front room. "Ready?"

"No." He gave me a lop-sided grin.

"Let's go." I opened the door, and we headed out.

It was only a couple of blocks up to the avenue and the newsstand.

The boy was holding up the paper, a tall stack of them on the ground near his feet. Surrounding him was a small crowd, jostling for their copies. Several stood to the side, reading, unable to wait.

"Paper! Get your paper right here!" he sang out.

Tommy broke into a run toward him, but I just kept walking. Part of me didn't want to know and part did.

Guess all of Tommy wanted to know.

"Mayor re-elected! Second term for mayor," the kid shouted, as other men and boys grabbed papers, tossing dimes into the kid's hat to pay for them.

My heart stopped, and so did I. Frozen. Afraid to believe it. Afraid to react. Afraid it was all a dream.

Down the block, Tommy skidded to a halt, his back to me. He dug in his pocket and tossed in a dime, then grabbed one of the papers from the stack. Guess he didn't believe the newsboy.

It was all I needed to hear. I closed my eyes and thanked God for listening to my prayer.

But Tommy stood there, reading.

I stood still, waiting for him.

He turned around, paper still in his hand, and looked at me. Then he smiled.

I smiled back.

Tommy tossed the paper down, and bolted to me. "Max! It's true!"

He reached me and launched into my arms. "Whoa!" I caught him and swung him around, then put him down fast before we drew any attention.

"This means we can stay!" he yelled.

"Sure does." I tousled his hair.

"And it means I can go back to Storyville!"

"Honestly, I'd rather you didn't. I don't like the idea of you playing in whorehouses. Listen, on the beat the other night I stopped at the Big 50 and talked to one of their musicians. You know that trumpet player?"

Tommy nodded. "Yeah. Louis? What about him?"

We strolled side by side down the block, back toward the house.

"Well, he says someone is opening a club on Bourbon Street. He thinks you might be able to get a job there with the band."

"Really?" Tommy's eyes shone so bright I thought I was looking at the sun. "When?"

"Don't know. But we can talk to him tonight."

"Great!"

We reached the house. *Our house.*

Mrs. Riley was on her porch and she waved to us. "Good morning, Officer O'Rouke!" she called.

"It's a great morning!" I called back.

"Is your friend staying?" She nodded at Tommy.

"He is. He's going to stay with me."

Tommy stared up at me, blinking his big blue eyes at me from behind those glasses.

"That's good. I'm glad you've found a friend."

"Me, too." I gave her a final wave and headed up the steps.

"Max," Tommy whispered as he followed me up.

"What?" I opened the door.

"You think she knows? About us?" He glanced back across the street.

"Maybe." I shrugged as I shut the door behind him.

"Do you think she'll report us?" He ran his hand through his hair.

"No. She loves hearing you play piano." I took Tommy into my arms. "Relax. We're safe. No Fallzone political ambitions. No one is going to report us. You'll get to play piano again. I'm still walking a beat in Storyville. Life's gonna be good, boy."

"You think?" Tommy held such hope in his eyes.

"Yeah, I do." I kissed him.

He grinned and said, "Then so do I." He broke away to throw himself down on the chair at the piano. He ran his hand over the keys, hitting each one with a flourish. The music burst out of him as I settled into my chair to listen to my boy play.

For now, everything was perfect. Tommy was safe and we were staying put.

I decided I'd take the exam for detective the next time it came up.

Hell, I didn't want to be a beat copper for the rest of my life and Storyville couldn't last forever.

About the Author

Lynn Lorenz is an award-winning and best-selling author who grew up in New Orleans but currently lives in Texas, where she's a fan of all things Texan, like Longhorns, big hair, and cowboys in tight jeans. She's never met a comma she didn't like, and enjoys editing and brainstorming with other writers. Lynn spends most of her time writing about hot sex with even hotter heroes, plot twists, werewolves, and medieval swashbucklers. She's currently at work on her latest book, making herself giggle and blush, and avoiding all the housework.

Locke & Blade (Locke & Blade of Waterford Patrol #1)

When Locke and Blade must work together to solve crimes, but will dislike turn to attraction in the heat of fighting their enemies?

Christopher Locke is a man with a tarnished reputation. When he's transferred to Waterford Station to serve as inspector, he meets Jonathan Blade, his new partner. Jonathan thinks Christopher is a brute. Chris thinks Jonathan is a snob. Both think the other is more than attractive, which might be more dangerous than the enemies they must face.

Cemeteries

Damned to forever travel the path he used to flee a powerful Voodoo Prince, Jacob falls for Mike, and together, they must decide their own destinies.

Damned to forever travel the path he used to flee a powerful Voodoo Prince, Jacob Foster has used many types of transport. Nowadays, he uses the bus. A particular bus marked CEMETERIES. When Mike Lawson gets on he's the first person to speak to Jacob ever. As they ride the bus, they fall in love, but once Mike learns the truth about Jacob, with that love be enough to withstand their destinies?

Coliseum Square

Can Mark Madison, tutor to the young son of Royal DuCote, solve the mystery surrounding the death of Luc's mother and will it destroy the DuCote family?

When Mark Madison flees his past, leaving his family and his name behind, he hires on as a tutor to the famous DuCote family in New Orleans. Inside the grand house on Coliseum Square, Mark discovers a mystery. The wife of handsome Royal DuCote died in an accident two years before and since then her young son Luc has refused to speak. Silence and sorrow rule the house and its inhabitants, but intriguing and handsome Royal DuCote wants his son to learn, despite his muteness. Mark makes it his mission to find out why the child won't speak and solve his muteness, but in doing so might just destroy what's left of the DuCote family.

A Miracle for Markie

Seven-year-old Markie is determined to shine this Christmas. He's decided his light can't be hidden any longer, but not everyone in his life is supportive.

This Christmas, he's looking for a miracle. Maybe if the family's Nativity can host a miracle, then it might spill over onto him and his family.

CPSIA information can be obtained
at www.ICGtesting.com
Printed in the USA
FSHW010447051019
62635FS

9 781641 222716